# Home Melody

A WHOLESOME CHRISTIAN ROMANCE
RHAPSODY OF GRACE BOOK 1

## Milla Holt

REINBOK LIMITED
*United Kingdom*

Copyright © 2024 by Milla Holt

All rights reserved. No part of this publication may be reproduced, stored in a retrieval system, distributed or transmitted in any form or by any means, without prior written permission.

Published by Reinbok Limited, 111 Wolsey Drive, Kingston Upon Thames, Greater London, KT2 5DR

Publisher's Note: This is a work of fiction. Names, characters, places, and incidents are a product of the author's imagination. Locales and public names are sometimes used for atmospheric purposes. Any resemblance to actual people, living or dead, or to businesses, companies, events, institutions, or locales is completely coincidental.

Cover by Willette Cruz

Editing by Sara Turnquist

Home Town Melody / Milla Holt. -- 1st ed.

ISBN 978-1-913416-26-3 Print ISBN 978-1-913416-27-0

# Welcome to the Mosaic Collection

**WE ARE SISTERS,** a beautiful mosaic united by the love of God through the blood of Christ.

Each month The Mosaic Collection releases one or more faith-based novels or anthologies exploring our theme, Family by His Design, and sharing stories that feature diverse, God-designed families. Stories range from mystery and women's fiction to comedic and literary fiction. We hope you'll join our Mosaic family as we explore together what truly defines a family.

If you're like us, loneliness and suffering have touched your life in ways you never imagined; but Dear One, while you may feel alone in your suffering—whatever it is—you are never alone!

Learn more about The Mosaic Collection at

www.mosaiccollectionbooks.com

Join our Reader Community, too!

www.facebook.com/groups/TheMosaicCollection

# Mosaic Collection Books

### MID-YEAR ANTHOLOGIES
Before Summer's End: Stories to Touch the Soul
Song of Grace: Stories to Amaze the Soul
All Things New: Stories to Refresh the Soul
Dancing in the Rain: Stories to Shelter the Soul
Sounds Like a Plan: Stories of Change and the God Who Doesn't

### CHRISTMAS ANTHOLOGIES
Hope is Born
A Star Will Rise
The Heart of Christmas
A Whisper of Peace
A Thrill in the Air

### JOHNNIE ALEXANDER
The Mischief Thief (Rose & Thorne #1)

### BRENDA S. ANDERSON
A Beautiful Mess
Pieces of Granite (Coming Home Series Prequel)
Broken Together (written with Sarah S. Anderson)

### ELEANOR BERTIN
Unbound (The Ties that Bind #1)
Tethered (The Ties that Bind #2)

Lifelines (The Ties that Bind #3)
Flame of Mercy
Flicker of Trust

**SARA DAVISON**
Lost Down Deep (The Rose Tattoo Trilogy #1)
Written in Ink (The Rose Tattoo Trilogy #2)
Every Star in the Sky (two sparrows for a penny #1)
Every Flower of the Field (two sparrows for a penny #2)
The Color of Sky and Stone (In the Shadows #1)

**JANICE L. DICK**
The Road to Happenstance (Happenstance Chronicles #1)
Crazy About Maisie (Happenstance Chronicles #2)
Calm Before the Storm (The Storm Series #1)
Eye of the Storm (The Storm Series #2)
Out of the Storm (The Storm Series #3)

**DEB ELKINK**
The Red Journal
The Third Grace

**CHAUTONA HAVIG**
Twice Sold Tales (Bookstrings #1)
Clock Tower Bound (Bookstrings #2)

## MILLA HOLT
Into the Flood (Seasons of Faith # 1)
Through the Blaze (Seasons of Faith # 2)
Within the Storm (Seasons of Faith # 3)
Amid the Ashes (Seasons of Faith # 4)
After the Frost (Seasons of Faith # 5)
Home Town Melody (Rhapsody of Grace #1)

## ANGELA D. MEYER
This Side of Yesterday
Where Hope Starts (Applewood Hill #1)
Where Healing Starts (Applewood Hill #2)
Where Joy Starts (Applewood Hill #3)

## STACY MONSON
When Mountains Sing (My Father's House #1)
Open Circle

## LORNA SEILSTAD
More Than Enough
Watercolors

## CANDACE WEST
Through the Lettered Veil (Windy Hollow #1)

## OTHER
Totally Booked: A Book Lover's Companion

To my husband, who is my biggest cheerleader, and my critique partners Kim and Rachael, who pushed me out of my comfort zone.

# Chapter 1

"THERE SHE COMES. SUPERMUM herself."

"Really? Where?" With a theatrical gasp, Adria Baines made a show of sweeping her gaze over the run-down neighborhood playground. "I need to ask her for some advice."

Adria's arms jolted as she pushed her toddler's stroller over the bumpy surface toward her best friend, Katie Mason.

The women hugged next to the swings, one of the few functioning pieces of play equipment left on the Meadow Hill housing estate.

Katie stood back, hands on her hips. "It's true, though. I don't know how you do it. I'd be shattered after an all-night shift flipping burgers. But here you are, fresh as a daisy."

"Fresh as a daisy?" Adria chuckled. "More like a gritty-eyed zombie. I don't know how I'll survive when this guy drops his afternoon naps. Thankfully, he still takes a big, long one. We've just woken up."

She stooped and unstrapped Owen, her twenty-two-month-old son, from his stroller.

"I'm not surprised he had a long nap. He was up at half-past five this morning," Katie said.

"Oh, no." Adria shot Katie a glance. Her friend always made an effort to look presentable, but her concealer didn't quite hide the dark circles under her eyes. "Did he wake you?"

On the nights when Adria worked, Owen slept at Katie's place and Adria picked him up on the way home. She was already pushing it, knocking at anyone's door at half-past six in the morning. She cringed at the thought that her son woke Katie's young family much earlier than that.

"No, he didn't wake us." Katie pointed at her toddler, Rose, who was kicking her plump legs in one of the playground's two swings. "Little Miss Energizer Bunny here was up at five. And she only does one short nap during the day."

"Mummy!" Owen bounced in his stroller, a stubby finger pointing at the swing. His little face blazed with excitement that would soon morph into impatience.

"Do you want to go on the swing, sweetheart?" Adria lifted him into the bucket-style seat of the toddler swing, kissing him on the forehead and ruffling his brown curls.

She gave the swing a big push, then turned to Katie. "You're the real Supermum if you're on the go all day. I depend on Owen napping for at least two hours."

Along with the precious hours of sleep she snatched between putting Owen to bed at Katie's place and the start of her overnight shift at ten, the little boy's afternoon nap gave Adria just enough rest to keep functioning. Barely.

And meeting Katie for their children's regular play date kept Adria sane. They'd been part of the same mother and baby group, two women in their early twenties bonding as first-time mums while swapping notes about nappy rash and nipple cream.

Katie, tall and rail-thin with straight red hair and blue eyes, had a perfect mini-me in little Rose. Adria, five foot three if she was being generous, was still using Owen as an excuse for the extra pounds that had moved in to stay. He had her dark curly hair, but his complexion was several shades lighter than her dark caramel skin.

They usually took their toddlers elsewhere rather than hanging out at Meadow Hill's grim playground with its rusty, broken-down equipment. Despite being part of Elmthorpe, a once-popular English seaside spot, Meadow Hill was almost four miles from the beach.

But Katie, who was expecting her second child, had a prenatal checkup today, which meant there was no time to walk or take the bus to a nicer park.

So, here they were. Adria looked around her. Spring was supposed to be the season of fresh green beauty. But in Meadow Hill, the warmer weather only meant more weeds forcing their way through the cracked asphalt and forming deeper tangles around the edges of the playground.

Adria gave Owen another push, smiling at his giggles. At least he enjoyed himself. And so did little Rose. There was someone missing, though.

"Have you heard from Bella lately?" Adria asked, pulling her jacket tighter around her.

Katie shook her head. "Nope. But I've seen a lot of Mike, lounging around like he owns the estate."

Adria made a face. Bella also lived in Meadow Hill, and she had been part of their mother and baby group. The three of them used to hang out together until, against Adria's warnings, Bella got back together with the father of her son.

Adria leaned toward Katie and spoke in a lowered voice. "I told social services he'd moved back in with Bella."

Katie stared at her, wide-eyed. "No, you didn't."

"I did. He shouldn't be around her or Charlie, but he keeps worming his way back. He nearly got her evicted because the neighbors are fed up with the loud music and screaming matches and people partying at all hours. There was none of that before he moved in. She'll lose custody of Charlie if he keeps hanging about. I thought if I told social services, they might give her the nudge she needs to finally get rid of him."

Katie twisted the end of her ponytail around her finger. "I don't know about that, Adria. Bella's made her own choices. She won't thank you for involving the social."

"She doesn't have to thank me. I don't mind being the bad guy as long as she and Charlie are safe. I'd rather have her hate me than stay friends while that jerk uses her as a punching bag because there's no food in the house after he's spent all her money at the bookies."

"I wish it hadn't come to that," Katie said. She pulled Rose's swing back and let it go.

The little girl erupted into laughter.

Katie turned her attention to Adria once more. "Enough about Bella. What's the latest news from the council?"

Adria groaned. "Don't get me started. I got a letter saying they've turned down my application to be rehoused. Apparently, they consider the cockroaches to be treatable, although they've been failing to treat them for the past two years because they won't talk to the guy next door. I'm sure the roaches are coming from his place. And they say that the mold is because of my lifestyle."

"You're kidding me," Katie said. "You're one of the cleanest people I know. Seriously, your place is spotless."

"Apparently, I'm the one to blame for that mold that won't go. I shouldn't hang so much washing in the flat. And I'm supposed to ask the neighbor's roaches politely not to come into my place without an engraved invitation." She had to joke about it. The alternative was to sit in her flat and cry in frustration.

"Do you know what I think this is all about?" Katie asked. "They just don't want to put their hands into their pockets and pay to fix the issue. I'll bet it's structural damage. It'll take some money to sort out, and that's why they're dragging their feet and hoping you'll just give up and go away."

Adria suspected her friend was right. Elmthorpe Town Council wasn't even keeping up with its most basic responsibilities, never mind fixing housing for social tenants. Her gaze landed on an overflowing bin that spewed garbage the way a fountain gushed water. Since the council cut down on trash collection, the bins got full quickly.

Perhaps the full bins were the council's job, but the garbage littering the playground was all about Meadow Hill's residents. As always, the smell of sun-warmed asphalt mingled with the scent of rotting trash. Ah, the unmistakable fragrance of spring.

"You know what really gets me?" Adria said. "If the issue is so treatable, why has it taken them almost two years to treat? How do I know they won't be tinkering around with it for another two years? I wish I could just ditch the place and find a private rental."

The swing had slowed to a stop, and Owen shifted restlessly.

Adria looked down at him.

He pointed at the motorbike-shaped spring rocker on the other side of the playground.

"You want to play over there, sweetheart?"

She took him out of the swing and set him on the ground.

He trotted to the rocker, lights flashing on his little sneakers. He loved those shoes so much that he'd insisted on wearing them to bed the first couple of nights after she'd bought them. Until she'd convinced him that the sneakers needed to sleep in their own little bed.

Katie gave Rose another push on the swing. "Since you brought up a private rental, I don't get why you won't get help from Owen's dad."

"I'd really rather not," Adria said. "It was just a one-time thing and I doubt he even remembers it. He was out of there so fast that he left a trail of smoke."

Katie rolled her eyes. "I know the kind. They disappear as soon as they get what they want."

"Isn't that the truth?" For a short while, Adria had fooled herself into thinking this guy would be different. He'd been sweet and funny, and then gentle and hesitant.

Then afterwards, he'd stared at her, ashen faced, as he grabbed his clothes. She could swear he'd been crying as he stumbled out of the room, mumbling, "This was a mistake. I'm sorry."

By the time two lines showed up on the pregnancy test, that guy and that night were long gone. And Adria had known she was on her own.

The shrill voices of an arguing couple filtered through an open window from a nearby apartment, shaking Adria back into the present.

"He's still responsible," Katie said. "Or at least he should be. I know you said you got nowhere trying to tell him about the baby, but I've got a phone number for a solicitor who should be able to help."

Adria snorted. "And what am I supposed to pay a solicitor with?"

"He takes legal aid. As a single mum trying to get child support, I think you'd qualify. You wouldn't have to pay anything. He'll do all the work, and Owen's father could at least help towards putting a decent roof over his head. What was his name again? Lucas?"

"Levi Falconer." The only reason she knew his surname was because it was written in a Bible, of all things—the one thing he'd left behind. Apart from the baby in her tummy, of course. She'd kept the Bible, thinking he might want it back. And even after the months passed and she'd hit a wall when trying to contact Levi, she'd still kept it.

Katie took Rose out of the swing. "Well, Levi might have ignored your calls, but he won't be able to ignore an official letter from a solicitor."

"I'll think about it."

The sound of helicopter blades filled the air.

From his motorcycle rocker, Owen squealed and pointed upward. "Copter! Copter!"

Adria shaded her eyes and squinted into the sky. It was probably the police on the hunt for some criminal or other on their estate. Owen was still young and innocent enough that helicopters were nothing but exciting. One day, his innocence would end and he'd understand the reality of the world he lived in. But not today.

She glanced at her friend, who looked at her with a strange expression.

"What's wrong?"

Katie sighed. "I was putting it off, but there's no easy way to tell you. Chris and I are moving. We just confirmed everything this morning. He's been offered a job in Kent and we've booked viewings on a couple of houses over there."

"No way! That's fantastic news." Like Adria, Katie and her husband were eager to leave Meadow Hill. "When do you move?"

"As soon as we find a new place, we'll give our one-month notice."

"Wow. That soon?" Katie would finally leave this dump.

Selfish worries crowded Adria's thoughts. Like how much she'd miss her friend. How would she carry on working without Katie to babysit Owen overnight?

She shoved those thoughts aside and reached out to hug her friend. At least one of them would escape Meadow Hill. "I'm so happy for you. Tell me all about it."

Over Katie's shoulder, she caught sight of Owen playing in the overgrown grass. He had something in his hands.

Adria's heart lurched. "Owen, put that down right now."

The sharpness of her tone startled him and he stared at her, wide-eyed.

Adria rushed forward and snatched the item from Owen's hand—a used syringe. Needle still attached.

Owen screamed, his face turning red.

"What is that?" Katie came up to them, her face paling as she saw what Adria held with her fingertips.

Katie pulled a wad of tissues from her pocket and wrapped the syringe in it. She wedged the bundle into the heap of rubbish that spilled out of the nearby bin.

Shaking, Adria hugged her sobbing child. Her heartbeat thudded in her ears. "Sorry for shouting at you, darling. That was really dangerous. It's okay now, sweetheart. It's okay. You're okay now."

Owen's weeping subsided into hiccups as Adria rubbed his back.

Random bits of drug paraphernalia were not unusual on this playground. Meadow Hill's dope heads probably hung out here more often than the estate's children. But Adria had never seen a needle around, just lying in the grass where her child could pick it up.

Her arms tightened around Owen. Even if she did get the council to sort out her substandard housing, there would still be the issue of her son growing up in a place like this, where his local playground had two pieces of play equipment that worked alongside needles and smashed liquor bottles and who knew what else.

Katie was leaving. It was time she did everything she could to get out of here, too.

She stood slowly, turning to face her friend. "Give me that solicitor's phone number."

ADRIA PUSHED OWEN'S stroller toward her apartment block. The building crouched its gray bulk on the edge of the concrete courtyard, looming over a dingy square like a neighborhood bully.

Katie was leaving. Her only friend in this miserable place would soon be gone. And her hands still shook after grabbing that needle from Owen. What if he'd pricked himself?

At least the usual group of idlers who loitered around the courtyard weren't here today. She wasn't in the mood to deal with catcalling and nonsense after the afternoon she'd had.

She sucked in a deep breath and held it as she approached her front door. The stairwell next to her ground-floor apartment always stank of vomit and urine, and she didn't want to inhale it if she could help it.

She pulled her keys from her pocket and opened the front door, pushing the stroller inside ahead of herself.

Adria released her breath only after closing the door. No matter what anyone else did out there, at least she could keep her home clean and safe. She could shut out the smells and most of the noise. Although, no matter how long and hard she scrubbed, she couldn't rid the apartment of the odor of mildew that clung to everything. Not unless the council finally did their job and fixed whatever was causing the damp.

She let Owen out of the stroller and folded it up, stowing it in the closet next to the front door.

# HOME TOWN MELODY

Singing softly, he toddled behind her as she walked toward the living room.

She froze, and he bumped into the back of her leg. A brick lay in the middle of the floor, surrounded by broken glass, soil, and shattered earthenware. And the remains of her window plants. A jagged hole in the window marked how the brick had come in.

Her heart pounding, Adria grabbed Owen's arm as he tried to walk past her.

Her phone buzzed with a text message.

**Pity about yr window. Thats what u get for sticking yr nose where its not wanted. Watch out. Sometimes, kids r hurt coz of there mums stupidity.**

There was lots more, describing her with the filthiest, most vulgar words and racial slurs.

Her hand trembled, but she kept a hold on Owen as he squirmed to get away.

It was Mike. It had to be. He'd figured out she'd called social services. He already knew Adria had tried to convince Bella to leave him. It wouldn't have taken much for him to put two and two together.

Adria could handle the dirty looks Mike and his cronies threw her way when she saw them around the estate. She could block out the insults, too. But they were threatening her son now and putting bricks through her window.

She could complain to the council until she was blue in the face. But what would the authorities do? Even if she could prove who had done this, after weeks and weeks, perhaps, they might give Mike an antisocial behavior order. A mere slap on the wrist that would do nothing to protect her and Owen.

She had to move out of Meadow Hill. To do that, she needed money.

The universe, or God, or whoever was out there, had sent her a message, and she was listening loud and clear. She would call that lawyer right now and find out how to get child support for her son.

# Chapter 2

Levi Falconer punched a fist in the air. The guitar in his hand hummed as the last resonant chord of his brother's newest song faded. "Guys, this is insane. Are you hearing what I'm hearing?"

He grinned at his two brothers as they sat facing each other with their guitars on their knees in the converted barn they used as rehearsal space.

This building, set away from the main house on the Falconers' hundred-acre estate, was the heart of their music ministry. The high vaulted ceiling, crisscrossed by exposed wooden beams, created the perfect acoustics, even with the windows open to let in a fresh spring breeze.

This was where the inspiration of art met the discipline of craft. Over countless rehearsal sessions across the years, the brothers' jam sessions blended into times of worship and prayer. It all crystallized into music in the dozens of albums whose artwork adorned the rough-hewn stone walls of the barn.

And now, Levi marveled yet again at his brother Ezra's songwriting talent. "This has got to be the lead single. What do you think, Zach?"

Zach, the eldest brother, flashed a smile that, along with his thick black hair and blue eyes, inspired magazines to label him "the handsome one" in their band. "I was leaning toward 'A Purified Heart,' but now I think this is my favorite of the lot. You've really done it this time, Ezra. We can take this straight to the studio next week."

Ezra inclined his head. With his stylish, swept back hair and well-groomed beard, he exuded an air of effortless cool. "Thanks, guys. I prefer 'A Purified Heart,' but I'll go with the majority."

Levi ran his hand through his own short-cropped dishwater brown hair, feeling a bit scruffy compared to his meticulously styled brothers. He didn't have Zach's sharp looks or the charisma that came as naturally to Ezra as breathing, but he was okay with that. Pouring his energy into being the work horse of the band suited him just fine.

He strummed the opening bars of the soulful ballad based on Psalm 27, which Ezra called "Strength of My Life." "It's agreed, then. We'll go with 'Strength.' I've been desperate to record new material after such a long time."

"Old music doesn't seem to have done you any harm," Ezra said, shooting a glance at Levi. "The royalty checks for your Christmas classics collection must be a comfort for the lack of original music."

Levi hesitated before answering. Ezra's humor was tart rather than sweet, and sometimes it was difficult to tell whether anything lay behind his words. Lately, more often than not, his quips veiled a barb, or something simmering under the surface.

Ezra's solo album, released six months ago, had critics in raptures over his original songs. But sales had been lower than expected. Meanwhile, Levi's album of familiar Christmas staples had been a runaway hit, making his solo venture the most successful of the three brothers', for anyone who kept tabs on such things. Which Ezra did.

Levi's fingers danced across the fretboard of his guitar, weaving his own twist into the riff between the chorus and verse of "Strength of My Life." It was probably best to ignore any undercurrent in his brother's words.

"Hymns and carols are nice, but I think everyone's looking forward to seeing the band back together with new music," he said. "Speaking of new, I'd like to hear how 'Strength of My Life' will sound if you and Zach swapped lead vocals." Ezra's more emotive delivery might be a better fit for the song's lyrical complexity than Zach's powerhouse voice.

Zach shrugged. "Sure, I'm happy to do that. But can we take five?"

"Make it ten, please. You're relentless, man," Ezra said. He turned to Zach. "Remind me again why we agreed to let our little brother lead rehearsals?"

"Because he thinks he's a drill sergeant and makes us actually work and stick to the program?" Zach asked.

Levi laughed. "Okay, okay. Ten minutes, then we'll try it again with Ezra on lead vocals."

Ezra and Zach set their guitars on nearby stands, then walked to the kitchenette on the other side of the room where Zach fished two bottles of water out of the mini-fridge.

"For what it's worth, I think you sounded amazing."

Levi spun toward the sound of the voice. He'd forgotten that their manager and publicist, Elaine Winchester, sat in on today's rehearsal. Positioned in a corner of the room, she'd been quiet until now.

"Thanks," he said.

She approached him with smooth, graceful steps, her ever-present tablet poised in a well-manicured hand. Wearing a tailored suit and with her blonde hair slicked into an immaculate bun, she looked out of place in the rehearsal room. But she knew all about the business side of the music industry and hadn't put a foot wrong in the three years she'd worked for them.

Levi credited her for bringing his and the band's finances back from the brink of disaster. Which was why she earned a hefty commission check every month and had his ear whenever she had anything to say.

Elaine swiped a finger across her tablet screen. "From what I've heard today, I'll be able to tell Charisma Records you're making progress, but they want firm dates for at least five meet and greets."

Levi groaned. He'd rather have a tooth pulled than do some of these promotional chores the record company wanted. The events where he got to meet the band's fans weren't so bad, but the industry mixers were the worst. "You mean we can't just concentrate on the music?"

"Afraid not," Elaine said. "The label expects you to pull your weight in pre-launch promo and right now, they don't think you're doing much pulling. Come on, throw them a bone so they'll be happy."

Ezra strolled up, water bottle in hand. "Why don't we look at our diaries and pin down some dates while we're all here together?"

"Fine," Levi said. "We'll get the boring promo stuff out of the way. But then we'll do the song immediately afterward."

Zach joined Levi, Ezra, and Elaine in a ragged circle, everyone tapping at their phones.

"Let's look at dates in May," Elaine said. "It's a pity we've missed the Easter events, but there are a couple of church conventions that I'm sure would be glad to have you make a guest appearance, even on short notice. Can we all block out the weekends of the 18th and the 25th? And in June and July we've got the cycle of summer camps and retreats. The biggest are Light the Flame in London and Brother's Keeper in Dorset."

As they marked off dates, the door opened and Beth Falconer stepped inside, smiling at her sons.

Elaine glanced around. "And we're done. That wasn't so painful, was it? It's amazing what we can do when we set our minds to it. I'll take these dates and build a promotional calendar around them. That should keep the label happy."

Mum walked toward the group. "I thought it might be time for a break, so I've put some tea and scones out at the house." She held up a letter. "Levi, this is for you. It just came by special delivery."

Ezra grinned at his younger brother. "What do you say, sarge? Scones first and then rehearsal?"

Levi sighed. "Fine. I'll read my letter while you all get some tea. But can we please be back here in thirty minutes?"

As everyone moved toward the door, he ripped the envelope open.

The words of the letter leaped off the page and punched him in the gut.

Levi Falconer, Falconhurst Manor, Hatbrook, Surrey

Dear Mr. Falconer,

Re: Preliminary Inquiry Regarding Child Maintenance Matter

I am writing on behalf of my client, Miss Adria Baines, regarding a matter of child maintenance concerning a child born on June 5th, 2022.

It has come to our attention that you may be the biological father of the aforementioned male child. My client and I are committed to resolving this matter amicably and without the need for formal legal proceedings.

Miss Baines informs me that the child was conceived on the night of September 10th, 2021, at the residence of James Caldwell in Padstow, Cornwall. My client was contracted as a house sitter and you were a guest of the owner of the residence. It is alleged that you and my client were intimate on this night, and my client retained an item belonging to you in her possession following your encounter.

While my client is confident in her belief regarding the child's paternity, we propose conducting a paternity test to provide conclusive evidence and facilitate a fair resolution of this matter. This will ensure that both parties have a clear understanding of their rights and obligations moving forward.

We understand that this may be a sensitive and significant matter, and we assure you that all necessary measures will be taken to ensure confidentiality and respect throughout the process. Our primary objective is to safeguard the best interests of the child and achieve a resolution that is mutually acceptable to both parties.

We kindly request your cooperation in this matter and invite you to respond to this letter within fourteen days to discuss arrangements for the paternity test and subsequent child maintenance proceedings.

Should you have any questions or require further information, please do not hesitate to contact me at the phone number or email address listed below.

Thank you for your attention to this matter, and we look forward to your prompt response.

Sincerely,

Henry Clark, Solicitor, Clark and Associates

"Levi. Levi! What's going on?"

Sharp voices added to the cacophony in Levi's mind.

A ring of faces surrounded him. Mum. Zach. Ezra. All staring at him as though he had sprouted a second head. When had he sat down on the sofa?

Someone pressed a bottle into his hand. In his other, he still held the letter, which flapped in his trembling fingers.

Zach took it from his hand.

Watching his brother's face, Levi knew the exact moment when the words sank in.

Zach stared at Levi, his face as pale as the sheet of pressed paper. "She got pregnant?"

"What?" Mum and Ezra said in chorus.

"Levi, please tell me what this is about." Mum's features were pinched. "What's in that letter?"

Levi scrubbed a hand down his face. How could he tell them about that night with the girl he met at his friend's house? The biggest mistake of his life. Even while giving in to the desire of the moment, he'd known that experiencing such complete openness and vulnerability, and the pleasure that came with it, was a gift only to be shared with the woman he committed to in marriage. Not snatched and stolen with someone he barely knew.

He'd left immediately, ashamed of what he'd done and determined to put it behind himself. But clearly it wasn't. Far from it. It was right here, right now.

Everyone was talking again, but Zach's soft-spoken question rang louder than all the other voices. "Could the child be yours?"

Levi took a gulp of water, but his throat still felt as if he had swallowed a mouthful of desert sand. "The timeline fits."

Mum grabbed the letter from Zach.

As she read it, Levi forced himself to look at her, to witness her dawning realization of how he'd failed to live by what he believed.

Finally, she raised her gaze to meet his. Her expression filled him with more shame and regret than he'd thought possible.

"Levi," she whispered, her eyes filling.

He blinked back the moisture in his own eyes. He'd broken her heart.

Ezra glanced at the letter over their mother's shoulder. "Wait a minute."

He shot a piercing glare at Levi. "Are you telling me that you fathered a child? And now the mother is coming after you for child support?"

Elaine had the letter in her hands now. The thing was doing the rounds nicely. Passing from person to person, exhuming his most shameful secret in its full stench and horror, and shattering his image as a man of integrity.

"I see," Elaine said, scanning the page. She was the only one in the room who appeared unruffled. "There is no evidence yet that the child is even Levi's. Unfortunately, people try this kind of thing all the time with celebrities."

She turned her gaze to Levi. "We need to get on top of this straight away. I advise you to get a family lawyer immediately. I know a few who are used to working with people in the public eye. If you want me to, I'll send you a list of three names you can choose from."

Levi stared back at her. Her cool, professional words made sense. But getting a lawyer would make all of this real.

Ezra walked to his brother. "Whether or not the child is yours, you've done enough to make this a possibility. Is that right?"

"Yes." That was the only fact that mattered. There was no point arguing that it had happened only once and that he was immediately sorry, spending the next hours praying through Psalm 51, confessing his guilt and recommitting his heart to God. His private sin was now public knowledge.

Ezra turned away, both hands shoved into his hair. "Lord, help us. And you knew about this, Zach?"

"It wasn't my story to tell," Zach said. "It was between Levi and the Lord."

"Well, now it's between a whole lot of other people. I don't believe this."

Mum put a hand on Ezra's arm. "Ezra, please."

She turned back to Levi. "I really want to meet the little boy. And his mother. We should invite them over to visit."

Elaine spoke up. "Respectfully, Beth, I think it's too early for that. I've seen this kind of racket play out before, when a person tries to score a big payday or fifteen minutes of fame by bringing a paternity suit against a celebrity. The first thing we need to do is engage a solicitor and call this woman's bluff by getting a paternity test from a lab of our choosing. Shall I move ahead with that, Levi?"

"No," Ezra said, glancing at Levi under lowered brows. "The first thing we need to do is speak with Pastor Noah."

The crescendo of their debate filled the room as they argued over what Levi should do next. Elaine's self-assured contralto clashed against Ezra's spirited tenor, while Mum's gentler but insistent tones resonated through the discord.

Levi's hand grazed his guitar, adding the dissonant hum of strings to the noise. They were supposed to be rehearsing their lead single and preparing for the album release. Not discussing the fallout of his moral lapse. Would there even be an album now?

He'd thought he could bury the shame of what he'd done that night. But it had screeched back to life to haunt him. This was his reality now. Humiliation and finger-pointing were consequences of his abysmal failure to live according to his beliefs. He'd better get used to it.

More importantly, he might have a child out there. He might be a father. He needed to find out for sure and face the consequences head-on.

"Stop it, please." Levi's voice sliced through the air, echoing through the instant silence. "Rehearsal is off, guys. Elaine, please go ahead and get me a lawyer."

# Chapter 3

Adria turned the small DNA sampling kit over in her hands, staring at the picture on the packaging. A gorgeous couple grinned at the camera, their ecstatic toddler sandwiched between them. As though anyone who needed to take a paternity test ever looked that thrilled.

She certainly wasn't beaming from ear to ear over having to prove that Levi Falconer was Owen's father.

Things had moved surprisingly quickly after her solicitor sent the legal letter. Within days, word came that Levi wasn't disputing the facts of their liaison, as his lawyer put it, and would be submitting his DNA sample for a paternity test.

When giving her the sample collection kit, her solicitor had told her, "Once paternity is established, you need to be prepared for the possibility that Owen's father might want contact with him."

Would Levi want to be part of Owen's life?

Judging from the way he'd taken off, mumbling some weird apologies and leaving no contact information, he'd intended their liaison to be one night only.

He'd turned up unexpectedly that September afternoon in Cornwall, as if blown in by the warm sea breeze, looking for his friend who owned the beachfront home she was house-sitting.

Every detail remained crystal clear in her mind—their long conversation while making and eating dinner together, the ridiculous Scrabble game where his spelling turned out to be even worse than hers, the hours spent binge-watching *My Little Pony* until two in the morning.

Then they'd hopped into the hot tub and started making out. What happened next just unfolded naturally, and she'd had no hesitation taking things further.

But it was like a switch flipped and he wanted nothing more to do with her after they'd been in bed.

In the days that followed, she'd run through several scenarios, trying to understand why he took off like that. Maybe he was married and cheating on his wife. Or perhaps he was just bored and looking for a bit of weekend fun with no strings attached. Either way, she was as disposable as a used tissue to him.

Then she'd done a Google search of his name and found that he was in a religious boy band. That explained the Bible he left behind and why he'd ghosted her after he'd gotten what he wanted.

She would have left matters there, chalking it up to a painful life lesson. But when she'd found out she was pregnant, she'd known she should at least tell him she would have his baby.

She'd gotten hold of a phone number for the band's manager and mustered the courage to dial it, asking if she could speak with Levi.

The woman who answered the call said Levi was busy with work commitments and had no time to take personal calls. "I'll pass along any message, but I can't guarantee he'll respond. Who shall I say is calling, and what is it about?"

There was no way Adria was going to tell a cold stranger on the phone about her night with Levi and her pregnancy. She'd just told the woman, "Please ask him to call Adria from Cornwall on this number."

Of course, he'd never called back.

But whether or not he'd wanted her to disappear, he had to support his son. And this little box with the oafishly grinning couple was the next step toward making that happen. She needed to take her DNA sample now, before Owen woke up from his nap. She'd wondered why she had to give a sample—wouldn't Owen's be enough? But her lawyer had explained that having the mother's DNA would make the results more accurate, since the lab would have Owen's complete genetic profile.

Following the instructions in the kit, she swabbed the inside of her cheek and put the swab in the vial. Time to get Owen's sample.

He was still asleep, lying like a starfish in his cot in the bedroom they shared. Her little piece of pure love and joy. Stroking his silky chestnut curls, she bent forward to kiss him.

"Time to wake up, sweetie." She lifted him out of the bed and held him close, his head nestling in the hollow between her shoulder and neck. Closing her eyes, she breathed in deeply the scent of him. He was everything to her. She'd do whatever it took to get him what he needed. Even going to Levi for help.

Owen was still heavy-eyed and rosy-cheeked when she ran the swab inside his mouth.

"All done, sweetie," she said, placing his sample into a fresh tube.

# HOME TOWN MELODY

She studied the packaging, scoffing again at the picture. There was no way this DNA kit would transform her, Levi, and Owen into the sparkly, shiny family on the box.

"Eliminate all doubts!" it said, and "100% Accurate!" Well, hopefully that part of the sales pitch was true.

Sealing everything into the prepaid postage box was straightforward. All she had to do now was post the package, and the lab would do its thing. Then she would get some help to give Owen the life he deserved.

Half an hour later, with Owen fed and strapped into his stroller and the package tucked under her arm, she stepped out of her front door.

Then she froze.

A group of young men stood loitering on the other side of the dingy courtyard, near the entrance. Mike, her friend Bella's lowlife boyfriend, held court in the middle of the bunch, dangling a joint between his fingers. She'd have to walk past them to get to the mailbox.

Adria's throat went dry as Mike's barking laugh rose above the hum of their chatter.

The housing officer from the council had given her an earful about replacing the window Mike had smashed. At least there had been no more vandalism and no more text messages. Perhaps he'd gotten his anger with her out of his system after throwing that brick into her apartment.

She kept her head down, walking quickly past festering puddles and patches of mildewing damp that lingered in the courtyard long after they should have dried. Not even the bright sun of a spring day penetrated into this place.

The group of men fell silent as Adria approached. She sensed their stares, but they did nothing to stop her. The entryway lay just feet away. She had almost passed them. Her heart accelerated as she kicked up her pace.

The toe of her shoe caught on a broken paving slab and she stumbled. The paternity test package flew from her hands, landing in front of a pair of brilliant white Converse sneakers. Her ears filled with the thunderous pounding of her heart.

As though in slow motion, Mike grabbed the package and straightened. He examined it, a smirk spreading across his face. "So, boys, what do you think this nosy little cow is sending to Heritage Genetics Laboratory?"

Adria gritted her teeth. "Give it back."

# HOME TOWN MELODY

"No way. Not until I get some answers." He shook the box. "What's this? You trying to find out you're related to some celebrity or something?"

His cronies guffawed, clearly overcome by Mike's wit.

Rage stewed within Adria. She made a grab for the package, but he held it just out of her reach.

He pulled a puff of his joint and blew the smoke into her face.

She stepped back. The last thing she wanted was to reek of pot. She pulled her phone from her pocket. "That's it, Mike. I'm calling the police and telling them you've stolen that."

"Who's stealing anything? I'm just being a concerned neighbor and sticking my nose into your business like you stuck yours into mine. As if I would want any of your trash."

"Yeah," one of his pals said. "Trash belonging to trash."

Mike snorted. "Absolutely filthy. In fact, it's making my hands dirty."

He tossed the package away with a flick of his wrist. It landed with a squelch in a puddle of stagnant rainwater.

Tears burning, Adria grabbed the box and wiped it with her sleeve. There was no way she'd let these idiots see her crying. She rushed out of the courtyard as Mike's laughter rang in her ears.

# Chapter 4

*L*EVI SAT ON THE edge of his bed, holding the sealed box containing his DNA swab. His father's smiling face looked down on him from a framed portrait placed atop his dresser. This was how Joshua Falconer was officially becoming a grandfather. Not from a son who married in openness and honor, but via a sordid secret encounter and confirmed in a lab.

What a mess he'd made. He threw the box onto his bed and buried his face in his hands. Thank God Dad wasn't here to witness it. But if Dad had been here, Mum would never have married Greg Monroe, and none of this would have happened.

Levi hated that his memories of his father were so few and vague, like a mist that slipped through his fingers the tighter he clung to it.

It was Greg who stood sharp in his childhood memories. Greg teaching him to ride a bike, how to cast a fishing line, and how to knot a necktie. Although Joshua had given Levi his first tiny guitar, it was Greg who'd stood and applauded in the audience when the Falconer brothers first played in public.

Ezra and Zach remembered Joshua teaching them many of their important "firsts". But for Levi, Greg held that place. Greg had stepped in as a father figure to Levi and his brothers, as a manager to their band, and as a husband to their mother.

He'd also stolen three quarters of a million pounds from the band and placed the Falconers' country estate in his name. The truth only came to light almost three years ago when Greg had crashed his car en route to the airport with his mistress. They'd had one-way tickets to Costa Rica.

As Greg lay recovering in the hospital, details of his duplicity seeped out, spreading like a slow, corrosive poison. Such as how he'd embezzled money meant to pay the band's corporate and Levi's personal taxes, and run up tens of thousands of pounds in credit card debt in Levi and his mother's names.

Reeling after learning he was still on the hook for the stolen tax money, Levi had dropped everything, jumped into his car, and driven for hours to his friend's home in Cornwall. Except James wasn't there. A girl had been house-sitting at the beach-front property. A very pretty girl.

Levi had wanted to forget his life. All his most precious memories had been tainted after Greg's betrayal. That night in Cornwall had all started with his overwhelming need to blot out his troubles and numb the pain.

And now there were new memories—Adria in the hot tub with her skin glistening in the moonlight, a heart-stopping kiss, the intoxicating lure of a physical connection that let him block all thought and just focus on the sweetness of her touch...and the bitter regret when it was all over.

Except it wasn't over. He looked at the package again. It wasn't over by a long, long way. And although he could try to rationalize what he'd done, no excuse could exonerate Levi from his own choices, nor the fallout from his actions.

What was it his pastor had said? You could apologize for being an idiot and trying to juggle with a chainsaw. But no matter how sorry you were, you still had to deal with the limb you'd lopped off.

He'd asked God to forgive him for being intimate with a woman outside of marriage. But now, he had to set things right. The first step in taking responsibility was to send his DNA sample to the lab.

Looking up at his father's portrait, he squared his shoulders. He was Joshua Falconer's son. Not Greg Monroe's. He would do his best to make Dad proud.

He picked up the blue box and passed through the large house and into the living room, making his way to the front door.

Mum stood in the entryway. She glanced up at him, scanning his face. "Are you going out? I was about to make lunch."

"Just to the post office. I'm going to drop this off." He held up the package.

"Is that—" She stopped, as if unable to complete her question.

"It's the paternity test."

"Oh, Levi." She squeezed his arm. "So, this girl... What's she like?"

Heat flooded Levi's face. He didn't have to guess who Mum asked about. "I don't really know her that well."

## HOME TOWN MELODY

He knew Adria could make a delicious stir fry out of random refrigerated leftovers and that Pinky Pie was her favorite character from *My Little Pony's* Mane Six. She was a better speller than he, and she hated strawberry Jell-O unless it had cut up bananas in it. Exactly the things you should find out about a woman before you slept with her and made a baby.

He tightened his grip on the test kit. "I'd better drop this off so it'll go out in the afternoon post. Don't hold lunch for me."

# Chapter 5

LEVI STOOD IN FRONT of the closed door at Grace Community Church, Hatbrook. Time for step two of his man-up-and-take-responsibility challenge.

The church building didn't have to be the venue for his talk with Pastor Noah Chaplin. He could have scheduled this meeting at a café or at the pastor's house. Noah would have been happy to come to Levi's home, as he had many times before.

But it seemed fitting that Levi come clean with his pastor here, in the place that had been his church home as long as he could remember.

He pulled the heavy door open and walked into the foyer. The hum of quiet voices floated through the air.

There was always something going on in the building. It was Tuesday morning, so the GCC women's book group would be gathered in one of the side meeting rooms.

But no, they were here, sitting in a circle in a corner of the foyer for some reason...and staring at him instead of the book they were supposed to be discussing.

Most of the regular church members had become used to seeing Levi and his brothers, who all worshiped here. Some of the old-timers had known Levi since he was a baby and had watched the boys grow up and become famous. But GCC was a growing church and there was still the occasional newcomer who gawked, open-mouthed, when they bumped into one of the Falconer brothers.

He nodded at the book circle. Would they all smile so warmly if they knew why he was here today? What would they whisper about when his secret came to light?

His DNA sample should have arrived at the lab by now, and his solicitor believed they could expect quick results, provided Adria had sent in the child's sample. He would know very soon if he was indeed a father.

But whether or not he was responsible for Adria's child, he needed to speak to Pastor Noah.

As a leader in the church's music ministry, Levi held the standing of an elder. He was expected to live a life of integrity. "Above reproach," according to the standards of Titus 1. He should have talked to Noah long ago, and not waited until there was a threat of his secret sin becoming known to all. Sweeping his weakness under the rug made him a hypocrite on top of his other failings. He was unqualified for ministry.

As he walked into the church office, Gladys, the pastor's secretary, met him with a beaming smile.

"Good morning, Mr. Falconer. Pastor Noah told me to send you straight in. But before I do, I wanted to thank you so much for putting in a good word for my Marvin."

What on earth was she talking about? Levi stared at her, his mind blank. Apparently, there was an entire world that still existed beyond the issues that had consumed his every waking moment since he'd gotten the paternity letter. But Levi had lost touch with that world.

He trawled his memory, groping for a flash of insight. Marvin, Marvin... Of course! Gladys's eighteen-year-old grandson. Terrible exam results on leaving school, at a loss about what to do with his life, but good with his hands and willing to work hard. Levi had recommended him for a job on the road crew with a touring Christian band.

Levi blew out a puff of air, relieved at remembering. Marvin was a keen, eager lad. Levi hoped he'd find his feet. "Did he get the job?"

"He did indeed." Gladys clasped her hands. "He's so excited about seeing the world. This job will be the making of him. I told him there's no shame starting at the bottom and working his way up."

Gladys's face was so luminous that Levi couldn't help grinning back. "I'm glad to hear that. Damascus Road are great guys with a fantastic team. And I know their tour manager will look out for Marvin. Say hi to him for me when you next see him."

"Thanks, but I'm not sure when that will be. He's already joined them in Bristol."

"Has he? Well, when you next talk to him, then."

"Will do." Her head bobbed with enthusiastic agreement. "I'll let you go in now. I took the liberty of making a carrot cake when I saw your name in Pastor Noah's diary. I'll bring in a piece for you when the tea brews."

Her thoughtfulness brought a lump to his throat. She knew he had a sweet tooth and how much he loved her carrot and walnut cake. This was yet another person who looked up to him who would soon learn the truth about what he'd done.

"Thank you," he said.

Levi's phone rang as he stepped toward the door. It was his solicitor, Oliver Sinclair-Smith, the one he'd engaged to handle the paternity suit.

He looked at Gladys, his heart threatening to hammer out of his chest. "I'm sorry, but I need to take this call."

"Of course, Mr. Falconer. I'll tell Pastor Chaplin you'll be a few more minutes."

Levi hit the answer button. This call could mean only one thing. There was news about the test. "Hello?"

"Good morning, Mr. Falconer. Do you have a moment?" Oliver's well-modulated tone gave nothing away.

"Yes, I do." Levi tightened his free hand into a fist. His life hung on the lawyer's next words.

"I am calling to inform you I have just received news from Heritage Genetics Laboratory. The paternity test confirms with a very high degree of certainty that you are the natural father of the child in question."

The world stood still, but Levi's head spun.

"This, of course, has many legal implications," Oliver said in his cut-glass accent, his voice as calm as though he were inviting Levi for a round of golf. "I'm available to speak with you at the earliest opportunity to go through what these implications are, to answer any questions you might have, and to discuss your next steps."

Implications. Somewhere out there, a little human being was running around with Levi for a father. Poor kid. Fathers were supposed to have their act together, to have a clue about life. Fathers didn't feel lost and unmoored, like they were teetering on the edge of the unknown, about to get pushed into the void.

He was responsible for a child's life. But what did he know about being a father? He could barely remember his real dad. And there was no way he was going to look to Greg as a role model.

"Mr. Falconer? Are you still there?"

Oliver waited for an answer. That meant Levi had to fill the empty space with coherent words.

He managed to get his brain and mouth working again. "Thank you for telling me. I'm on my way into another meeting right now, but I'll make an appointment with you as soon as I can."

"Not a problem, Mr. Falconer. I'll look forward to your call."

# Chapter 6

Somehow, Levi made it into Pastor Noah's office.

His pastor approached him with a smile, which morphed into an open-mouthed stare. "Levi, are you all right?" He closed the door behind Levi, then motioned him toward a set of armchairs grouped around a table.

"Are you all right?" Noah asked again.

"Not really, no." Levi sank into the chair.

He'd always looked up to Noah. The pastor, in his early thirties, had been classmates with Zach. But with his black hair and unlined features, people often assumed Noah was closer to Levi's age.

Noah was the kind of guy who would sit up all night with a grieving family, holding vigil at their loved one's deathbed, and then preach a rock-solid sermon the following morning. Since taking the reins as lead pastor after his father retired, Noah's deep faith and compassion had quickly made him a cornerstone of their community.

Levi counted Noah as a friend, but he hadn't told him about his one-night stand because he'd dreaded his pastor's disappointment. Well, now it was all going to come out. He'd better savor his final moments as a man of integrity in his pastor's eyes. Once he confessed, Noah would never see him the same way again.

Noah took a seat opposite him and leaned forward, his eyebrows drawing together. "What's on your mind?"

"I've just found out that I have a son." There. He'd ripped the Band-Aid straight off.

Noah's mouth fell open.

A moment of perfect silence passed, like the split second of quiet between knocking a glass over and it shattering on the floor into a thousand razor sharp shards.

Noah's voice was calm when he finally spoke. "I see. Shall we pray together before we do anything else?"

And that, too, was typical of Noah. Praying first before he launched into anything. How much trouble could Levi have escaped if he'd done the same thing?

Noah clasped his hands and bowed his head. "Father, thank You for giving us this time to speak together as friends and brothers in Christ. Thank You for Your love for us. We ask for wisdom as we have this talk. Please help us both to open our hearts and to truly listen to each other and to You. Above all, we recognize that You are in charge in every situation, and we trust You to show us the right thing to do. Amen."

"Amen," Levi whispered.

"How did all this happen?" Noah leveled a searching gaze on Levi. But he wasn't throwing up his hands in disgust the way Ezra had. He just looked as if he cared.

Levi pushed a hand through his hair. "It was when all that stuff blew up with Greg."

He didn't need to tell his pastor what a devastating time it had been for the Falconers. Noah had been right there throughout the whole ugly process of Greg's arrest, trial, and conviction.

Levi drew in a slow breath. "When I found out the Revenue Office was coming after us for the tax money Greg stole, I felt as if the walls were closing in. I needed to just get away. It didn't matter where to. I left my phone behind, got into my car, and began driving."

When Levi had realized his aimless driving had got him onto the M4 motorway, he'd decided he might as well drive to the very tip of England until there was no more road.

"I have a friend who lives in Cornwall, and I thought it would be the perfect place to silence all the noise in my head. When I got there, he wasn't home, but there was a young woman house-sitting. I told her James was my friend. She called him to confirm it, and he said I could stay.

"She made dinner, and we talked for hours about all sorts of things, but nothing important. It was such a relief to chat with someone who knew nothing about me. Someone who wasn't pitying me or full of outrage about Greg. It was so easy and peaceful being around her. One thing led to another, and we ended up in bed together."

Levi hung his head. "I immediately regretted what I'd done, and I got up and grabbed my things and left."

"So there was no question of a relationship with her?" Noah asked.

"No. I never expected to see her again. I didn't even know her second name." How terrible did that sound? Exactly as bad as it was.

He'd slept with a girl whose surname he didn't know. To fulfill his own selfish desires. And then he'd run off like a coward after getting what he wanted. She didn't deserve to be treated like that.

Levi scanned Noah's face for any sign of revulsion, but saw none.

It was such a relief to let the whole story out. "The entire way back home, I asked God to forgive me. I told Zach, but no one else. Mum needed all of us to be strong for her, so I boxed the whole incident away in my mind and carried on with my life.

"I recorded the Christmas album because I needed to make some money fast after what Greg had done. Thank God it did really well. Greg went to prison, our finances were back on track, and I thought everything was behind me.

"Then a few days ago I got a letter from Adria's solicitor, saying she'd had a child. I did a paternity test and just before I came in, I found out the baby is mine."

That was it. There was nothing more to tell. He couldn't sink any lower.

Noah leaned forward, resting his elbows on his knees. "You've been under an incredible amount of strain. The situation with Greg, the financial scare, the affair, the baby. Any part of it would be a lot to deal with. How are you coping?"

The question caught Levi off-guard. It was the first time anyone had asked about his wellbeing. He hadn't expected it because he didn't deserve such concern.

"I...I don't know." His throat thickened painfully. "I'm just putting one foot in front of the other. I'm ashamed of how I handled myself. Sick of how I let everyone down. It's just sinking in that I'm a dad and I have to figure out how to be a father to this child. And co-parent with Adria after the way I treated her."

She had been completely open and vulnerable to him. He had used her, taking something from her to which he had no right. How did she feel about what he had done? She probably resented him.

"What's going to happen next with the child?" Noah asked. "What did you say the name is? And is it a boy or a girl?"

Heat seared Levi's face. "A boy. But I don't know his name. I'll meet with my solicitor—tomorrow if possible—to talk about what to do next and how I can see him."

"Does your family know?"

"They were with me when I got the letter from Adria's solicitor. But they don't know the paternity test results. Ezra's worried about how this will affect our album launch. To be honest, though, that's the last thing on my mind."

"What's the first thing on your mind?"

"Seeing my son. Working out some sort of arrangement with Adria. Somehow making amends to her. And getting my life as a Christian back on track." There was no way Levi could handle this mess without God's help.

Noah nodded slowly. "Can we talk about the last thing you mentioned? About getting your life as a Christian back on track?"

Before Levi could answer, Gladys knocked and came into the room with tea and the promised carrot cake.

Levi gripped the arms of his chair as Gladys fussed around with the cups and saucers. Never had a living being taken so long to put out two teacups and lay out two slices of carrot cake. Would she ever be done?

Gladys finally flashed a warm smile at Levi. Remorse hit him like a stab in the gut. She was just trying to be kind. The only reason she'd brought the cake was because she knew he liked it. Used to like it. All food went down like sawdust mixed with ground glass now.

When she left, Noah leveled his gaze on Levi once more. "We were talking about your walk with the Lord."

Levi swallowed. Was this the part when Noah told him he'd be dis-fellowshipped?

Noah said, "Sexual sin is something many Christians struggle with. You're far from alone. The most important thing I want to know when someone is caught up in sexual immorality is where their heart is. Are they feeling a conviction, a desire to change and to live out their sexuality within the boundaries God ordained? Or are they determined to carry on in unrepentant sin?"

There was no question in Levi's mind. "I want my heart to be right with God."

Noah's eyes warmed. "I believe that. It comes across strongly in everything you've told me. That's why I don't think it's necessary to go through the process of formal church discipline. We only do that when someone is determined to pursue a lifestyle that's not in line with God's will."

He paused for a moment. "You're already on a path to restoration. You've taken the first and most important step by asking God to forgive you. But I sense there's still some way to go. For one thing, there's Adria.

You mentioned wanting to make amends to her. I think that's another good indicator of where your heart is."

Levi's gut twisted with fresh guilt. "The truth is, I've tried my best to blot her out of my mind. I haven't faced up to how I wronged her. Even my own repentance has been pretty self-centered."

Leaning forward, Noah squeezed his arm. "Sometimes—very often in fact—God deals with things in stages. We get to grips with one issue, and then He brings something else to light. It's a journey. And speaking as your pastor and your friend, I'll support you and walk with you through this."

"Thank you." Levi blinked back tears. He'd been dreading this meeting. He should have known Noah would react with nothing but grace.

"However, you'll have to step down from your leadership position in the church."

Levi took a deep breath. He'd suspected this was coming. He couldn't carry on leading others in his church when his own personal life was an utter mess of his own doing. "I should have stepped down as soon as I got back from Cornwall. I'm sorry that I didn't."

Noah's shoulders relaxed. "I'm glad you're on board with that. I'm not saying you can never serve again. This isn't a punishment. It's to allow you space for reflection. You'll need time to address the issues that led to this, as well as your new life situation. And, as I said, I'll support you in every way I can."

"I appreciate that." Noah's words made sense. Space to deal with his issues was exactly what he needed. Plus, it would be a relief not to have to stand in front of everyone, leading them in worship while feeling like a hypocrite.

"Give me a moment to think." Noah stood and walked to the window, standing for a moment with his back to Levi. His head was bowed as though he were praying.

Finally, he turned around. "There is one more thing. If it was just a question of what happened between you and Adria, that's where the matter would rest, since it's over and you're clearly repentant. No one else would need to know unless you decided to tell them. But...there is a child."

Levi swallowed. Where was Noah going with this?

Noah spread out his hands. "I'm thinking about the wider church family now. Since you intend to be an active part of this child's life and you're clearly a single father, I would strongly encourage you to tell our church members so as to avoid rumor and speculation."

"Tell the church members? What do you mean?"

Noah looked at him the way a doctor did when they were just about to inflict an agonizing shot.

"I want to be very clear that this is not meant to publicly shame you. We don't want GCC people seeing you with your child and gossiping and guessing about how he came into the world. We need our church family to understand that we take sexual purity seriously. But even when we fall short, we can still repent and be restored, and your little boy is a precious life to be received and welcomed among us."

Levi took a deep breath and blew it out slowly. So, it would come out. Of course it would. An entire human being existed because of his actions and there was no way he was going to keep his son hidden. He just hadn't realized there would be a PSA in front of the congregation...everyone looking at him while he told them about his one-night stand.

But Noah's reasons made sense. It would be better to put the information out there before people started whispering and wondering.

Levi squared his shoulders. "All right. I'll tell the congregation."

"Excellent. We can work out how to do that later. Or I can do the talking if you're more comfortable with that." Noah glanced at his watch and groaned. "I'm so sorry to rush you out. If I'd known ahead of time what the situation was, I'd have cleared my morning schedule. But someone else is coming to see me in about ten minutes and I want us to take some time to pray before that."

"That's all right. I'm very glad I came," Levi said.

Although Noah now knew his failings, and the church would, too, Levi felt a lot better than he had in a long while.

"I haven't told my family yet about the test results. Please pray about that, too."

"Of course. Let's pray now."

# Chapter 7

ADRIA PUSHED A SHOPPING cart along the baby and toddler aisle at her local Aldi supermarket.

Owen bounced on his perch at the front. He was still so easily delighted with the simplest of pleasures, like sitting in the cart on their weekly trip to the grocery store.

She tickled the velvety soft skin under his chin, making him squirm and giggle.

His needs would soon outstrip her slender budget. Hopefully, she'd soon get help with that.

Adria walked past the branded products, scanning the upper shelves for the store's own-brand nappies. The price of pull-ups had gone up yet again. It was crazy how much they charged for a pack of just ten. At these prices, it made more and more sense to start potty training. But Owen wasn't showing any signs of being ready.

Her phone rang as she grabbed a jumbo pack of pull-ups.

The caller ID showed Henry Clark, her legal aid solicitor. Her pulse quickened. He must have news about her paternity suit.

"Hello?" she said, tossing the nappies into the cart.

"Good morning, Miss Baines. Is this a good time to talk?"

"Yes, now is fine." The supermarket wasn't the ideal place to conduct legal business, but there was no way she was waiting to hear what he had to say.

"Excellent. I received word from the Heritage Genetics lab this morning, and their tests confirm that Levi Falconer is the father of your child."

Although she was certain that Owen was Levi's son, Adria closed her eyes and let out a slow breath. Somewhere, deep inside, she'd had an irrational fear that something would go wrong with the test and it would show a weird result. But she had proof of the truth now.

Her fingers trembled as she gripped the handlebar of the cart. "What happens now?"

# HOME TOWN MELODY

"Well, soon after I got the lab results, I heard from Mr. Falconer," Henry said. "He wants to meet with you and the child."

Adria's heart froze as she glanced at Owen. "Meet us? Do you think that's a good idea?"

"It's a reasonable request on his side. Naturally, he'd like to see his son. Presuming you have no fears for your or the child's personal safety, I see nothing against having an informal meeting with Mr. Falconer in order to break the ice and form some sort of rapport. Do you have any reason to fear for your safety?"

Adria's mind went back to Levi and the evening she'd spent with him, alone in a house in Cornwall, miles away from the nearest neighbor. It hadn't even crossed her mind that he might be dangerous.

"No, I'm not afraid for our safety."

"In that case, as long as you make no agreement or undertaking, verbal or otherwise, it should be fine to meet with him. In fact, I encourage it."

"All right," Adria said. "Did he say where?"

"He proposes that you and the child have lunch at his family estate in Surrey this coming Saturday."

"His family estate? Do you mean he wants us to go to his home?" She'd expected him to suggest somewhere neutral. Not where he lived.

"Yes. His mother will be there, too. I took it to be a sign of good faith that they're inviting you into their family home."

"I...I guess that's okay."

"Excellent. Falconhurst Manor is a couple of miles outside of Hatbrook. And, as I said, he suggested this Saturday. Would that suit you?"

She had to work on Saturday night, and Surrey was a couple of hours away by train. It might be a bit of a hassle making all the connections, but she could be back at Elmthorpe in time for her shift. "Yes, that'll be fine."

"Good. I'll inform him and be back in touch with the necessary details in due course. Enjoy the rest of your day, Miss Baines."

"Thanks," Adria said, and ended the call.

She was going to see Levi again. Years after their night together, after he'd ghosted her and ignored her attempts to contact him through his manager. She was under no delusion about his interest in her. Their evening together meant nothing to him, and the only reason he was responding now was because Owen was his.

She raised her chin. That didn't matter. All she wanted was for him to provide for his son. But she'd have to get used to the idea of making room for a father in Owen's life.

Owen stared up at her, his brown eyes wide and clear.

She touched his cheek. "Well, little man, you're about to meet your dad."

# Chapter 8

LEVI PACED UP AND down the lounge of his home. Somewhere out there, a car was bringing his son closer to him with every passing second. Owen. He'd made sure his solicitor found out the boy's name. Any moment, he would see and maybe even touch his child.

And then there was Adria.

Levi stopped his pacing and stared out of the window. He had wronged her, first by using her as a means to meet his own need. And then, after taking that precious intimacy, discarding her as if she were insignificant. Even if a child hadn't come out of it, the fact remained that he had treated her shabbily. And he had no idea how to tell her how sorry he was.

Mum came into the room holding a basket of toys.

"Where did you get those?" Levi asked, grateful for the distraction.

Mum had gone into overdrive the minute she heard Adria and Owen were coming. No detail escaped her attention, from planning the menu to agonizing over which room in the house they'd use to entertain them and whether she should get a gift for Owen. And if Owen got a present, should she get one for Adria?

Levi finally got her to settle on using the smaller, cozier lounge where the family hung out, rather than the big living room they normally reserved for more formal occasions. And he'd talked her out of getting gifts for either Owen or Adria. Too many things could be read into a gift. There'd be plenty of time for presents later, once they got to know Owen better.

Mum put the basket on the floor. "I was rooting around in the cellar looking for some of your old toys and books. I hadn't realized I'd kept so many."

He smiled as he looked at her flushed face. Of course, she was excited. She was about to meet her first grandchild.

He crouched in front of the basket and picked up a faded yellow plush. He chuckled. "You kept my Pikachu?"

"Of course I did. You'd have rioted if I'd thrown it out."

The housekeeper, Mrs. Moore, appeared in the doorway. "Excuse me, sir, madam. I've just got word from security at the gate. They've let a taxi through and it's on its way up to the house."

Levi rose as Mum straightened.

"Thanks for telling us," she said. She made for the front door with quick steps.

He followed her, suddenly wanting a few extra moments to prepare himself.

As he stepped outside, a white cab was just pulling around the turning circle. It stopped in front of the main entrance.

The driver got out, nodded, and went to the trunk.

The passenger door opened on the far side and a young woman emerged.

It was her. That flawless, warm brown skin with a dusting of freckles that reminded him of cinnamon sprinkled over a cappuccino. Her curly dark brown hair was piled on top of her head in a messy bun now, but he'd seen it tumbled around her shoulders. He'd buried his hands in it while he kissed those lush lips. As she reached back into the car, her wide-necked cable-knit sweater slipped to the side, exposing a shoulder that he knew was as soft as a rose petal.

The memories Levi had held at bay for almost three years assaulted him like a baseball bat to the head. Reeling, he hung back while Mum rushed forward.

Adria lifted a small child from the car. His son. A cascade of silky chestnut curls framed the little boy's face, the dark hair contrasting with his tawny skin. That sordid night, the one Levi wished he could erase from memory, had brought about this perfect little boy.

Owen glanced at Levi. His large, expressive eyes—mirrors of his mother's—were fringed with impossibly long, black lashes. His gaze, direct and innocent, reached right into Levi's soul.

Mum held her arms out. "Welcome! My name is Beth. I'm so glad you could come."

"Hello. I'm Adria and this is Owen." Her voice, quiet and husky, triggered a fresh avalanche of memories.

Levi's feet carried him forward as though drawn by a magnet.

Owen's gaze dropped to the Pikachu plush Levi still held.

Levi raised the toy and, after another searching stare, Owen reached for it.

The little boy curled a small arm around the toy and hugged it to his chest, his head resting on his mother's shoulder.

A movement just to the side caught Levi's attention.

The taxi driver held out a folded-up stroller to Adria. "There you go, miss."

Levi stepped toward the driver, speaking to the others over his shoulder. "Why don't you all go inside? I'll settle the tab."

Adria rummaged in her purse with her free hand. "No, that's okay. I've got this."

"Let Levi take care of it," Mum said, touching Adria's shoulder. "Come on."

Adria glanced in Levi's direction, stopping just short of meeting his eyes. "Thank you."

Levi's gaze followed her as she walked away. She'd gained some weight since they'd met. And she wore it so well. She was even more beautiful than he remembered. He squeezed his eyes shut. This was going to be a really hard day.

The cab driver coughed, and a wave of heat scorched Levi's face as he fumbled for his wallet.

## Chapter 9

Adria followed Beth Falconer onto the porch, walking between an imposing pair of tall columns. Beautifully trimmed shrubbery in stone planters lined each side of the entryway.

The place screamed money. It looked like one of those massive houses in the period dramas Katie binge watched on Netflix, where everyone lived on vast country estates and spent all their time having fancy garden parties.

Beth blended right in, with her expensively styled hair, designer slacks, and cashmere twinset and pearls. Adria glanced down at her own jeans and cable-knit sweater. She should have worn something more formal. What on earth had she been thinking?

Adria felt even scruffier when she stepped inside the house. This was the kind of interior design people showcased in glossy magazine pages.

# HOME TOWN MELODY

A man who lived in a place like this came from a completely different universe than the one in which she slogged through night shifts in order to keep a mold-ridden roof over her son's head. This was probably another reason why, after their night together, Levi had taken off as if the hounds of hell were after him.

Beth led her into a large room. Light poured through the floor-to-ceiling windows.

"Sit anywhere you like," Beth said, gesturing toward a three-piece suite arranged around a gleaming oak coffee table. The chairs were draped in burgundy velvet.

Adria chose the end of an L-shaped sofa. Although it looked so expensive and pristine that she was afraid to sully it, the seat was deliciously comfortable, the overstuffed velvet cushions giving her a welcoming embrace as she settled Owen onto her lap. She glanced at his hands. He'd had a snack of cheese puffs in the cab. Had she got all the orange dust off his fingers?

Levi came into the living room a moment later and she sneaked her first proper look at him, taking in his lean runner's build. He wore a dark blue button-down shirt with the sleeves rolled up. That must be his favored look—he'd had a shirt like that in Cornwall. She'd liked it then, too. Although his brown hair was a lot shorter and his skin more tanned, she could have picked him out of a crowd of thousands.

She hadn't yet seen the smile that had first drawn her to him. It was a smile she'd never forgotten. How could she? He'd passed it on to Owen.

Levi didn't look at her even once as he settled into an armchair. When his gaze came in her direction, it veered away from her and locked onto Owen.

"Was it a long trip down from Essex?" Beth asked.

Adria's face heated. Had Beth noticed her checking out Levi?

She cleared her throat. "It took about two and a half hours, but we were lucky with the connections. We didn't have to wait too long between trains. It helped that there was only one change."

Owen leaned forward, and Adria followed his gaze. He stared at a box of toys on the floor in front of Levi's chair.

"Do you want to look at those, Owen?" she asked.

He nodded, and she put him on the ground. He walked to the box and tugged at a plush rabbit.

"Those belonged to Levi and his brothers," Beth said. "I went digging in the cellar today and found them. Wasn't that bunny yours, Levi?"

"It was Ezra's." He was watching Owen's every move, as though he couldn't get enough of the little boy.

Owen dug some more and found a plastic sheep.

Again, Beth's voice pulled Adria away from looking at Levi looking at Owen. "I made some lunch for you, but I probably should have asked whether you or Owen have any food allergies."

Adria shook her head. "No. Owen can eat anything."

"All right. I won't be a minute." She walked out, leaving Adria, Levi, and Owen in the room.

Levi slipped onto the floor and sat next to Owen. He picked up the toy sheep. "Do you know what a sheep says? Baa."

It was a very convincing imitation, and Owen smiled.

Levi picked up a cow and waggled it in front of Owen. "Moo. Do you know what? I used to have a whole farm of these. Shall we find all the animals?"

Levi rummaged in the basket and got out a pig and a horse.

Owen stuck in a hand. He pulled out another sheep, adding it to Levi's line of animals.

Levi picked up a figure of a man wearing a large straw hat. "This is the farmer. Do you think his name is MacDonald?" He began to sing. "Old MacDonald had a farm. E-I-E-I-O. And on that farm, he had a cow. E-I-E-I-O."

It was the same ridiculous childish song she'd heard and sung herself a million times, but his melodious voice made the skin on the back of her neck tingle.

"With a moo, moo here, and a moo, moo there. Here a moo, there a moo, everywhere a moo, moo. Old MacDonald had a farm. E-I-E-I-O. And on that farm he had a..." Levi paused, looking at Owen.

After a moment's hesitation, Owen pointed at the pig.

Levi's grin lit up his face. "And on that farm, he had a pig. E-I-E-I-O."

When the pig was dealt with, Owen pointed at a sheep. They cycled through the animals, and by the time they came to the final chicken, Owen's gaze was fixed on Levi instead of on the toys.

Beth came back into the room balancing a tray of glasses and a crystal pitcher containing a pale yellow drink. Ice cubes clinked against the sides, while lemon slices floated gracefully on the surface.

She set the tray on the coffee table, beaming as she took in the sight of Levi and Owen on the floor. "You've got all the farm animals out. You used to play with those for hours, Levi."

Beth turned toward Adria, gesturing at the pitcher. "I made some elderflower cordial. My boys loved it when they were little. We used to go out and forage for huge bunches. Do you remember, Levi?"

"Vaguely," Levi said.

"It's a bit too early in the year for elderflowers, but I found some I'd kept in the freezer. I thought Owen might like to try some, but I've also got water. Or milk, if you think that's more suitable." She frowned. "I probably ought to have asked you about that, too. I know mothers are much more conscious about sugar intake and things like that these days. We hardly gave that sort of thing any thought when I was raising my boys. This is a rather sweet drink."

"Elderflower cordial would be lovely, thanks. I'm just amazed you can make a drink out of wildflowers," Adria said.

As Beth's face relaxed, Adria sat up straight with a sudden thought. Maybe Beth was as nervous about this visit as she was.

Beth filled a Thomas the Tank Engine sippy cup. She screwed the top on and handed the drink to Owen.

The child was the center of attention as all three adults watched him take a long pull from the cup. He smacked his lips, then took another drink.

Levi laughed. "I think he likes it."

"That's a relief," Beth said, smiling. She joined Levi and Owen on the floor.

Adria sipped from her glass of cordial, savoring the fruity taste and the fresh tang from the lemon.

Owen guzzled his own drink, flanked by his father and grandmother, the focal point of their adoring gazes.

Her son had a family now. She glanced around at the beautiful living room. A family with money. What would happen if the Falconers decided they wanted to take Owen away from her? Would she be able to stop them?

# Chapter 10

Levi held back a smile as Owen's pudgy fingers grappled with the last chunky piece of a wooden jigsaw puzzle. He could almost hear the wheels turning in the little boy's head.

The play of emotions across his child's face fascinated Levi. A tiny frown creased Owen's forehead and he pursed his pink lips as he turned the puzzle piece around.

Mum stretched out a hand, but Levi held her back. "He's about to figure it out. Give him a moment longer."

Owen's frown deepened as he tried to wedge the piece in the wrong way around.

"You were almost four when you did that puzzle," Mum said. "Owen isn't even two yet."

"He's smarter than I was. Look, he's getting it."

Owen fitted the wooden giraffe's head onto its torso, glancing up as the three grownups around him burst into applause.

"Well done, sweetheart," Adria said, her voice yanking Levi's gaze to her face.

A smile lit her features, reminding him why he'd avoided looking at her all afternoon. The sight of her beckoned his mind into dangerous places. He was going to have to learn to school his thoughts. Either that or treat her like the sun and never let his gaze rest on her.

Owen mirrored Adria's delight, stepping to her as he pointed at the completed puzzle.

"You did it. That was brilliant." She scooped him up into a hug, holding the boy close.

As Levi watched them, his arms ached to hold his little boy. He'd missed almost two years' worth of baby cuddles. He was wrong for how he'd treated her. But her actions weren't blameless, either. She'd kept him in the dark about his son.

Adria wrinkled her nose as she held Owen. "Seems you were working on something else besides that puzzle."

# HOME TOWN MELODY

Mum sat back on her heels. "Do you need to change his nappy?"

"Yes, please. Is there somewhere I—"

"Yes, of course. The bathroom is through that way, the first door on your left. You know what? Why don't I show you?" Mum stood, smoothing out her slacks.

Adria rose as well, balancing Owen on her hip as she picked up her nappy bag. "Thanks."

As she stepped past him, Levi caught a whiff of Owen. Ugh, that was pungent proof that there was more to parenting than playing with his son. He'd missed out on the reeking nappies as well as the fun times. Why had Adria waited this long to tell him he was a father?

Throughout the afternoon, they'd limited the conversation to surface-level small-talk while fussing over Owen. But questions were growing in Levi's mind. Why was Adria's first contact with him via a lawyer when his child was almost two years old? Perhaps she had kept his son from him because she resented the way he'd left after their night together. Could she have thought someone else was Owen's father? Surely not. That thought stank worse than a full diaper.

Mum came back into the room, her hands clasped over her heart. "Owen is an absolute delight. And Adria seems like a rather nice girl. A good mother, too."

Levi was in full agreement about his son. He wasn't so sure of Mum's assessment of Adria, though. "How can you tell?"

"How can I tell what? That she's a nice girl, or a good mother?"

"Both."

Mum stooped and grabbed a handful of toy blocks that were scattered on the floor. "The way she handled herself with Owen. He minded her when she told him no, but he wasn't afraid to explore and look at new things. She's very attentive to him and it's obvious they have a really close bond."

Owen did seem to be a very happy, healthy child. And Adria was responsible for that as he'd had no input whatsoever.

Adria came back into the room as the clock on the mantelpiece chimed. Her eyes widened. "I didn't realize it was getting so late. We'd better get going. I want to catch the 6:40 train to London Bridge."

Mum's expression fell. "So soon? Won't you stay for dinner?"

"That's very kind of you, but I need to get back home. I'm working tonight."

Levi stared at her. "You work at night?"

"Yes. I do the overnight shift at a fast food place near home."

"And where's Owen while you're out all night?" Levi realized the sharpness of his tone only when Mum laid a hand on his arm.

Adria raised her chin, her eyes hardening. "He stays over with a good friend of mine and her family."

Mum's grip on Levi's arm tightened, a sure sign that she wanted him to watch his mouth. "I'm glad to hear that you have such support," she said. "But if you're going to work tonight, we'd love to offer you a ride home."

Adria glanced at Mum, her shoulders relaxing. "It's fine, really. I'm prepared to go back by train."

"Please. I insist. It's such a long way. It'll take you, what, almost three hours to get back? Including train changes and waiting on the platform?"

Adria's hand crept up to tease a loose curl at the nape of her neck. "Something like that."

Mum said, "Our driver, Phillip, will take you. He has family living up in Colchester, and he can use the chance to drop in on them. It'll be a win-win-win. Phillip will see his family, you won't have to go by train, and I'll feel a lot better." She stood. "No more argument."

Adria's lips curved upward and the lines of her face softened. "Thank you."

"I'll let him know."

Mum left the room, and Adria let Owen back onto the floor.

He made for the basket of toys as she sat on the edge of her chair, arms crossed.

Silence hung in the air, only broken by intermittent electronic beeps from Owen's toy phone.

Levi cleared his throat. "So, how long have you lived in Essex? Elmthorpe, was it?"

She glanced at him, then looked away. "I moved there a couple of months before Owen was born."

"So, you weren't staying in Elmthorpe when we...when we met."

"No." She angled her body away, her attention seemingly on Owen.

Levi fell silent. This whole situation was upside down and wrong. There were things he knew about Adria that no man except her husband should. And yet here he was, wearing a mask of politeness and asking her the most banal questions.

Forget this nonsensical small talk. He needed some answers from her about things that really mattered. He'd already put his foot in it by challenging her childcare arrangements, so he might as well carry on and ask what was foremost on his mind.

"Why didn't you tell me you were having a baby?"

Her head snapped up, and her gaze locked with his. "What?"

"Why didn't you tell me about Owen earlier, when you found out? Why did you wait until now?"

A flush stained her cheeks. "You're the one who never called me back. I left three or four messages with your management team."

That was not the answer he expected. "My management team? Who exactly did you speak to?"

She glanced at Owen, who was now engrossed with pushing a Thomas the Tank Engine toy around a wooden train track. Lowering her voice, she said, "I talked to a woman who said she managed your band. I don't remember what her name was."

Did she mean Elaine? "And you told her about the baby?"

"No. I couldn't say that to a stranger over the phone. I left my name and my number and asked them to tell you to call me about an important matter."

Levi stared at her. Could she be telling the truth? If she was, that meant someone hadn't passed her messages to him. He'd have to find out from Elaine. If Adria had called, Elaine or her assistant might not have realized that she wasn't just a random fan. But they should have at least let him know, especially if Adria had called three or four times.

"So, you really never got my messages?" Her eyebrows drew together.

He shook his head. "No."

"I was almost ten weeks along when I first found out. When I didn't hear back from you, I thought you were avoiding me. So, I let things lie."

Could he trust what she said?

There was still one question niggling at him, though. "If you thought I was avoiding you and you were going to get on with your life, what made you contact me now?"

Her blush deepened, but she held his gaze. "Because Owen needs more than I can give him. I'm a single mother with no qualifications working for minimum wage in a fast food restaurant."

In other words, she needed money. Her honesty struck a chord deep inside him.

There was no shame in needing support. She was young and hadn't planned on having a baby. He was financially stable only because God had blessed him beyond his dreams. And Owen was his son, his responsibility to provide for. Adria should never have been struggling on her own to meet his needs.

The silence lingered a beat too long as he stared back at her. Her clear, brown eyes held depths that a man could easily lose himself in.

He shook himself before they drew him in any further. "Thank you for bringing Owen today. I want you to know that I'll do my part. My lawyer will be in touch shortly with a proposal about how to move forward."

At the mention of the lawyer, something shifted in her expression. It was as though shutters had come down over her eyes, and she looked away.

Mum came back in the room lugging a car seat. "I took the liberty of picking this up when I heard you were coming. I believe it's the right size for Owen."

Adria's eyebrows went up. "Wow, thank you."

"You're welcome," Mum said. "And Phillip says he'd be absolutely delighted to drive you two home. He's bringing the car around now. His daughter and grandson live in Colchester. Are you close by there?"

"I think we're about forty or forty-five minutes away," Adria said. "It takes about that long on the bus."

Mum put the car seat down and touched the basket of toys and books. "And please take as many of these as you want. I don't think he's going to let go of that Pikachu."

Adria smiled at Owen, who had kept the Pokémon plush close by all day. "Time to go home, darling."

# HOME TOWN MELODY

Levi grabbed the car seat and Owen's stroller, then headed outside. He needed something to do with his hands until he could make sense of his brief conversation with Adria. Merely two minutes of speaking with her had stirred up a storm in his mind and heart, leaving him with a tangled mess of emotions and thoughts to unravel.

Phillip had already pulled the silver Lexus SUV to the front of the house.

"My grandson has one of these," he said, taking the car seat from Levi. "I'll put it in for you."

Levi walked around to the trunk and put the stroller in just as Mum and Adria came out with Owen.

Adria settled Owen into the car seat and turned to Levi. "I almost forgot to give you this."

She reached into her large tote bag and held something out to him.

It was his old pocket Bible. The one he used to keep in his glove compartment. Where had she—?

"You left this behind in Cornwall."

He stared at her, and then back at the Bible. Left it behind? The words of the paternity letter from her lawyer sprang back into his mind. *My client retained an item belonging to you in her possession following your encounter.* The "item" was his Bible. He'd forgotten to grab it in his mad rush to get away.

How fitting in a sad, ironic way. In all his dealings with her, he'd also forgotten every value this Bible taught him, by which he'd wanted to live his life—integrity, purity, courage, and honor, all had fallen by the wayside. Shame seared his face like a red-hot iron brand.

Adria turned to Mum. "Thanks for having us."

"It was our absolute pleasure," Mum said, stepping forward and hugging her.

Mum didn't do polite side hugs. Hers were full on, hearty embraces that made you feel wrapped up in a cocoon of warmth, welcome, and acceptance.

Adria's eyes widened and her face reddened as her arms went around Mum.

"Have a safe journey back, and I hope to see you again soon," Mum said.

Adria stepped out of the hug, her face still red. "Thank you."

Clutching his Bible, Levi gave her an awkward nod.

She nodded back, then turned to Philip. "Should I sit in the back or—"

Philip smiled. "Oh, either is fine. Maybe sit in the back with the little one so he doesn't get nervous."

"All right," she said, facing Mum again with a small wave. "Bye."

And they were gone.

Levi's chest ached as the car went down the driveway, taking his son away. A chunk of his heart was heading down that road. There were a million things he didn't know about what his future would look like, but one thing was clear. No matter what it took, he would be a real father to that little boy. Not just a DNA contributor or a monthly support check.

Adria had reached out to him because she needed money. He would provide all the support she needed, but it was going to be on his terms. He would do right by his son.

Mum wrapped her arms around her body. "I miss him already."

"I can relate." He set an arm around her shoulders as they headed back toward the house. Levi couldn't begin to guess what it meant to her to see her grandchild. At least she could enjoy the little boy without the crushing guilt and regret that plagued Levi.

Her face grew troubled. "I just hope we'll be able to see him often. They live so far away."

"I'll get in touch with my solicitor and discuss a way to keep Owen in our lives."

"How will you do that?"

Levi stroked his chin. "We'll have to make her an offer she can't refuse."

He stepped aside, allowing Mum to go through the front door first. "That reminds me. Elaine suggested that I engage a P.I. to find out a bit more about her."

"A P.I.?" Mum's eyes widened. "Is that really necessary?"

"She's the mother of my child and I know next to nothing about her," Levi said. "Like this stuff about working the night shift while Owen stays with a friend of hers. We don't know whom she associates with. Elaine's suggestion took me aback at first, but the more I think about it, hiring a P.I. seems like a sensible thing to do."

Mum frowned but didn't reply.

Levi said, "I'm going to be there for Owen. And I need to know exactly whom I'm dealing with."

# Chapter 11

ADRIA SNIFFED THE AIR in her spotless apartment. Despite hours of cleaning and a sandalwood and white jasmine reed diffuser, the odor of mildew still lingered. Levi was sending someone to discuss his child support proposal and he or she would be here any minute.

Opening a window sometimes helped dilute the moldy smell, but more times than not, it only masked the mildew by adding the stench of weed-laden smoke and whatever else the neighbors might be burning. She'd done all she could.

The doorbell rang as she straightened a throw cushion, causing her to jump and drop the pillow on the floor. She put it back in place and rushed to the door.

A tall, elegantly dressed woman, her smooth blonde hair in an immaculate chignon, stood just outside. The way her finely sculpted nose wrinkled, Adria was certain the woman detected all the unsavory scents around—from the vomit and urine in the apartment block stairwell to the creeping reek of mildew inside Adria's flat.

The woman's lips stretched in a mechanical smile as she held out a slender hand. "Adria Baines? I'm Elaine Winchester, Levi Falconer's manager."

Adria took the offered hand. Once, years ago, on a school trip to Colchester Zoo, she'd been allowed to stroke a boa constrictor. Adria had expected the reptile's skin to be clammy or slimy, but it was cold and dry. Elaine's hand felt just like that snake.

"Please come in," Adria said.

Elaine stepped inside, glancing around the apartment. Her gaze landed on Owen, who sat in the corner, absorbed with a pile of nesting cups. She stared at him unblinking for a long moment the same way those experts on the Antiques Roadshow assessed a piece of pottery. What kind of person looked at a child like that?

"So, this is your son. He's a very attractive child." Turning away, she sat on the very edge of Adria's sofa and placed her briefcase on the coffee table. "You certainly played your cards exactly right."

"Excuse me?" Adria walked to an armchair.

Ignoring Adria's question, Elaine snapped open her briefcase and pulled out a folder. "Let's get straight to the business that brought me here. Mr. Falconer's solicitor has prepared a proposal for child support."

She slid the folder across the table, toward Adria.

Adria opened it and removed several sheets of paper.

"I'll talk you through the main points," Elaine said, settling a pair of glasses on her nose and studying what must be her copy of the document. "Mr. Falconer will provide monthly maintenance payments for your son until the boy is twenty-one years old or out of full-time education. The payments will begin at £4,000 and will be adjusted for inflation in January of each year. He will fund your son's education but would like to have some input on where the boy studies. In addition to the maintenance payments, you will also be provided with a monthly stipend for any other incidental expenses."

Adria stared at the figures. This was beyond any level of support she had even dreamed of asking. She'd only hoped for something she could put toward renting a better home, but the amount of help Levi was proposing would change Owen's life.

"Okay," she said, trying to keep her voice level.

# HOME TOWN MELODY

"This offer is under the condition that you sign a non-disclosure agreement prohibiting you from revealing the details of your and Mr. Falconer's relations and the circumstances under which the child was conceived."

"What does that mean? Is that a gag order?"

Staring over the rims of her spectacles, Elaine fixed her gaze on Adria. "Not exactly, since this would be an agreement between you and Mr. Falconer. But it does mean that if you want to receive the very generous maintenance package he's offering, you may not speak of the details already mentioned. If you break the agreement, there would be penalties that might include losing the support and paying financial damages and legal costs. Confidentiality is very important to Mr. Falconer."

Adria frowned. Not that she was planning on blabbing to anyone, but did this prevent her from talking about her own life? She ran her gaze down the first page of the document, stumbling over the dense verbiage. This was way out of her depth. And there were several more pages of the same stuff. It wouldn't be smart to agree to terms she didn't understand.

"Do I have to sign this right away? I'd like to show this to my solicitor."

"Fair enough." Elaine removed her glasses and folded them into a leather case. "There's also another matter, which is completely separate from the child support."

"Okay."

"Mr. Falconer owns a two-bedroom property on the grounds of the family estate. It's completely detached and self-contained. Mr. Falconer is offering you a long-term rental lease to the property, with a nominal payment of £1 per month. He's asked me to make it clear to you that this tenancy offer is open to you, whatever you decide on the maintenance agreement."

Levi wanted her and Owen to live at Falconhurst? And practically rent free? She could get out of Meadow Hill. Owen could grow up on those beautiful grounds, far away from bullies like Mike and this crime-infested place. That was all she'd wanted when she started this process—to get a decent roof over Owen's head in a safe neighborhood.

A glance at Elaine's face soured Adria's excitement.

The woman looked at her as though Adria was something she'd scraped off the bottom of her patent leather Louboutin stilettos.

Elaine closed her briefcase and got to her feet. "You'll find the tenancy agreement for Falconer Lodge in your folder."

Adria stood, trying to match Elaine's poise. "All right. I'll be in touch soon with my decision."

Elaine swept another glance around the room, taking in Adria's well-worn, mismatched furniture and lingering on Owen playing in the corner.

She faced Adria again, a mocking smile twisting her glossy pink lips. "You know, I've got to hand it to you. You're a very clever girl. You picked the right guy to be your baby daddy and set yourself up for life. Now that you've successfully got him on the hook, please don't keep Mr. Falconer waiting too long for an answer. I'll show myself out."

Heat swelled in Adria's chest, but she couldn't think of a suitable comeback as Elaine headed toward the door.

Was this the kind of person Levi worked with? His driver Phillip had been friendly and respectful, even when he pulled the Lexus into her rundown neighborhood. She'd expected at least common politeness from his manager. She'd never met the woman before. So, why was Elaine so hostile?

# Chapter 12

*L*ATER THAT AFTERNOON, ADRIA hurried along Elmthorpe High Street, pushing Owen's stroller down the uneven sidewalk. Her solicitor had been kind enough to squeeze in a meeting with her on short notice and she didn't want to be late.

She really needed his take on Levi's child support proposal. It looked like a very generous offer, but what if she missed something? People didn't throw money around like that without expecting something in return. Or they got you hooked on the handouts and before you knew it, they were calling the shots in your life.

Maybe she was only suspicious because of the messenger Levi had sent. If Elaine Winchester handed her a briefcase with a million pounds, the first thing Adria would do was look for a concealed bomb. There was no way she would sign any agreement that woman had touched until Henry looked it over.

# HOME TOWN MELODY

Henry's office sat between the pound shop and a clothing store. She glanced up at the shuttered windows. Or, at least, it *had* been a clothing store. Like so many other businesses in this town, Flirty Fancy Frocks lay empty now, a "closed" sign hanging askew in its dusty door.

She navigated the stroller through the narrow entryway into Henry's office. The modest sign above the door was easy to miss—Adria herself had walked by countless times without realizing a lawyer's office was tucked away here. It blended into the background, much like Henry himself. But she trusted him implicitly, sensing a kind and honest heart beneath his stiff exterior.

Henry's receptionist ushered her straight through.

The lawyer, dressed in a three-piece suit even at this time of the day, stood to greet Adria. "So, things are moving in this child support case. Let's have a look at these documents Mr. Falconer's agent gave you. I'm rather surprised they didn't send them to me first."

"Do you think it's because he's trying to pull a fast one?" Adria handed him the folder Elaine had given her.

"I'll not make any conclusions until I see what his offer is." He settled a pair of horn-rimmed spectacles on the bridge of his nose.

Adria sat in a chair opposite as her solicitor read the documents. The glasses magnified his eyes, exaggerating his already owlish look.

What would he make of the child support offer and tenancy agreement? If Levi's lawyers had buried some terrible clause under all the legalese, Henry would sniff it out.

Owen became restless and Adria rummaged in the basket under the stroller, pulling out one of his favorite board books. It was about farm animals and each page had surprise pictures hidden under flaps and a button he could push to hear the animal noises.

Owen grabbed the book with a grin.

Levi had made wonderful animal noises for Owen on their visit to his place. He did it without looking embarrassed, going all in with the clucking, barking, and oinking. Was he used to hanging out with children? He flashed into her mind whenever she sang Old Macdonald to Owen now. And whenever she read Owen his farm animal book.

Could she take Levi's generous offer at face value, without worrying something may be behind it?

Henry turned the sheets over one by one, running a thick finger across each line. His face gave nothing away. He didn't appear fazed, either by what he read or by the soft backdrop of animal sounds from Owen's book.

Finally, he put the last paper away and blinked at her. "This is an unusually free-handed offer of child support."

Adria blew out a breath. "So, it's more than what you would have asked for?"

"Yes, well above what I'd considered proposing. Mr. Falconer appears willing to provide very well for his child."

"The money will be life-changing for us," Adria said. "But what about the non-disclosure agreement he wants me to sign? Should I be worried about that?"

"I see nothing objectionable in it. As an artist in the religious community with a public reputation to maintain, it's not unusual that Mr. Falconer would demand an agreement like this."

"So, you're saying this is a standard thing?"

"Yes, especially for someone in Mr. Falconer's position." Henry removed his glasses. "People who are in the public eye often require NDAs in situations that involve their private affairs. The person who breaches the agreement by sharing protected information would face significant financial penalties. For example, an NDA would deter somebody from selling their story to the tabloid press or writing a tell-all book that might jeopardize the celebrity's livelihood."

"That makes sense, but I'm not planning on doing any of those things." Did Levi really think she was going to approach some gossip magazine and spill all the juicy details about their time together? The thought had never crossed her mind, no matter how broke she'd been.

Henry smiled. "I didn't think you would, but Mr. Falconer and his solicitors don't know that. They're just being cautious and trying to protect his interests. My advice to you is to accept the offer. The terms are exceedingly generous, and the conditions refer to actions you have no intention of doing. May I be the first to congratulate you on such a positive outcome? Your son will be very well provided for."

"Thank you." So, Levi's offer was just as good as it sounded. No secret sting in the tail. She could finally let herself feel relieved and hopeful about Owen's future.

Henry tapped the document. "With child support agreed, the next step in a case such as yours would be to discuss contact or visitation arrangements between the child and the non-residential parent. Mr. Falconer has made no explicit mention of this, but he has proposed that you and Owen live on the Falconer estate, once again on extremely generous terms. Will you be taking up residence there?"

"I haven't fully made up my mind, but I was leaning toward moving there."

Adria worried her bottom lip between her teeth. She was desperate to move out of Meadow Hill. With Katie heading off to Kent, there was little tying her to Elmthorpe, or even Essex, for that matter.

Falconhurst was a beautiful country estate with the kind of grounds people paid money to visit on a day out. The fresh air and open spaces would be ideal for Owen. And, financially speaking, the move was almost too good to pass up, costing her only a pound a month in rent. But would it be awkward to live on Levi's family estate?

Still, it was a chance worth taking. If things became uncomfortable, Levi's generous support payments would more than cover the cost of renting elsewhere.

She met Henry's gaze, her decision firming. "Actually, no, we will move to Falconhurst."

He nodded once. "In that case, given your unique circumstances, since you will be living on the same estate as Mr. Falconer, I believe it would be best to allow contact between him and Owen to develop naturally, rather than trying to enforce a rigid schedule from the outset. Owen's best interests are paramount. If you and Mr. Falconer allow yourselves to be flexible and adapt to Owen's needs, this would probably yield the best outcome."

Talking to Henry was like having a conversation with a dictionary. She needed to make sure she understood him. "So, you mean instead of working out a plan of how much time Owen should spend with his father, we should just play it by ear?"

"Exactly. Living on the estate makes it easier for Owen to see his father naturally, without the pressure of scheduled visits. It's often best for the child's well-being to let these interactions happen organically."

Adria glanced at Owen, who remained engrossed with his animal book. "I suppose that sounds like a good idea."

"If you agree, I'll write a formal letter to Mr. Falconer's solicitor proposing that you and Mr. Falconer allow contact between him and the child to develop naturally. That would also show that you are as reasonable with contact as he is generous with his financial support."

Adria twisted a lock of hair around her finger. Isn't this what she wanted when she'd started this whole process? She'd hired a lawyer to go after Levi for child support. And Levi had promised he would "do his part." Doing his part apparently meant giving her a bunch of cash and a place to live for next to nothing.

She should be thrilled. It was a wonderful offer and said a lot about Levi and his commitment to step up for his son. She just wished it hadn't come through Elaine. Did his choice of a messenger say something about him, too?

Henry spoke again. "If this relaxed contact arrangement doesn't work out, you could always seek legal advice. I'm just a phone call away."

"All right," Adria said, pulling the documents toward herself. "In that case, I agree. I'll sign the papers and you can send him the letter."

# Chapter 13

Levi pulled his phone out of his pocket to check the time and instead stared at his new wallpaper—a picture he'd snapped on Saturday. That mop of silky chestnut curls, those wide brown eyes, so innocent and trusting—his little boy. When would he see Owen again? And would Adria accept his offer and move to Falconhurst?

His solicitor believed that £4,000 a month plus almost-free housing was a generous amount that any reasonable woman would be happy to receive. If it wasn't enough, Levi would find a way to give her more. Removing her financial burden was the least he could do for her. Adria shouldn't have to be working night shifts at minimum wage in order to support his child.

But the way she set him on edge, it would be wise to limit his exposure to her. The sight of her, the sound of her voice, conjured up images and memories he'd rather keep buried. Falconer Lodge was far enough from the main house and the grounds were so extensive that he didn't need to actually see her unless it was to pick up his son or drop him off.

Elaine cleared her throat.

Levi dragged his gaze away from Owen's precious face to look at his manager.

Lips pursed and one eyebrow raised, she stared at him. She was waiting for him to deal with a list of questions, none of which he was in the mood to answer.

She tapped on her tablet. "The news about your child is a ticking PR time bomb, and we can't delay putting out a statement much longer. We need to decide what and when to tell the record label, your fans, and the brands you represent."

Levi rubbed his forehead. Elaine was right. He was lucky to have her cool head around, focusing on his business interests. He couldn't seem to concentrate on anything apart from his messy private life. "I know. But I can't make any kind of public statement until I've settled things with Adria."

"I hope she'll be reasonable and sign the NDA," Elaine said. "Getting that locked down will go a long way toward plugging potential leaks so we can control the narrative."

Control the narrative? Her words snagged on his conscience like burrs sticking on a sweater. It sounded like something a manipulative politician would say. Not someone who was in Christian ministry. But Elaine was a seasoned publicist. He was way out of his depth, but she knew how to handle things like this.

She was an efficient gatekeeper, handling not just his public communication, but screening all strangers who wanted access to him.

Levi frowned. Like handling calls from strange girls who tried to contact him after meeting him in Cornwall.

"Elaine," he said, "Adria said she tried to reach me through my management team about two and a half years ago. Did you ever take a message for me from her?"

Elaine blinked at him as though thrown by his random change in the subject. "Take a message from Adria? No. Why would you think that? Did she say she spoke to me?"

"No, she didn't say whom she spoke to."

"I'm sure I'd have remembered. Adria is such an unusual name." Elaine tapped her chin with a red-lacquered fingernail. "You know, now that I think about it, I had a temp filling in as my assistant some two and a half years ago. Her work was unsatisfactory in several ways. Perhaps she was the one who took Adria's call."

Levi crossed his arms. "So, you're saying that due to your assistant's incompetence, I wasn't told I was becoming a father?"

"She was just a temp. She was a disaster and I complained to the agency who sent her. But it's shocking to hear she might have caused you so much harm."

Levi's phone rang before he could respond. The caller ID showed Oliver Sinclair-Smith, his lawyer.

Heart ramming his chest like a sledgehammer, he answered. "Hello?"

"Good morning, Mr. Falconer. I've just sent you an email with the details, but I'm calling to draw your attention to it. Miss Baines has accepted your maintenance terms, including the NDA. She also sent over a proposal for how to handle contact with Owen going forward."

Levi motioned to Elaine to give him a moment. His PR machinations could wait. He needed to see what Adria had to say about his visitation with Owen.

He headed to his office, his phone pressed to his ear. "I'm going to check my email now. What's in this proposal?"

"It's a rather interesting proposal, if I may give my opinion. Through her solicitor, she's asking that contact between you and Owen develop naturally, since you'll be living in the same compound. She thinks an unstructured and flexible arrangement might work better than trying to impose a top-down visitation schedule off the bat."

Levi opened his email and found the message from his solicitor. The idea of an organic relationship with his son appealed to him, but the lack of structure was unnerving. It left him with no standard to hold Adria to. "What do—"

A movement in the doorway caused Levi to glance up.

Elaine had followed him into the room.

He stiffened. His office was his private space. Even Mum knew to knock before she came in. He'd decorated it with the things that meant the most to his musical career. A signed Keith Green LP that once belonged to his father hung on one wall, and his first guitar hung on another. He ought to have closed the door behind himself.

He closed his eyes, pressing the phone closer to his ear. "Sorry, Oliver. What do you think about Adria's proposal?"

"I think it's sensible, especially given the unusual living arrangements that will be in place," the solicitor said.

"You do?" Levi would have expected his buttoned-up solicitor to want to spell out every detail and eventuality of a custody agreement. Not to recommend an ad hoc visitation arrangement. "What if it turns out that I'm not getting a reasonable amount of contact with Owen? I've heard horror stories where people make up reasons not to allow the other parent access to their child."

"I suggest trying it," Oliver said, "but I also recommend that you document all interactions with Miss Baines in case you need to seek a formal contact schedule in the future."

Okay, so he could keep a record and if things went south, the legal route was always open. "All right, I'll go with it. Please let them know. And thank you."

"My pleasure, Mr. Falconer. Goodbye."

Levi ended the call, excitement building. Owen was coming to stay. He'd have a chance to build a relationship with his son.

Mum would be delighted. She was dying to decorate Falconer Lodge for Adria and Owen, but he'd convinced her to wait until it was confirmed that they would be moving.

"I take it that was about Adria and the NDA?" Elaine's pale blue gaze was on his face.

"Yes, that was my solicitor. Adria's going to sign it. She's also proposed a flexible visitation schedule, which, in theory, means I can see Owen whenever I want."

Elaine nodded, her expression unreadable. "I did my best to let her know it was in her best interests to sign the agreement. It's a great offer and she's a smart girl, so I'm not surprised she went for it. And that means we've neutralized a potential loose cannon. That's great news as we figure out our PR strategy."

Neutralized? Adria was the mother of his child, not a national security threat. Elaine approached the situation as if orchestrating a military campaign rather than managing a public relations effort. And yet, that was a mark of her expertise, and the reason Levi needed her help. She marshaled her PR resources with the strategic precision of a seasoned general.

Levi stood. "Let's go back into the living room."

Elaine took a step toward the door, then turned. "Speaking of neutralizing loose cannons, is there any further news from the P.I.?"

Levi motioned for Elaine to lead the way into the hallway. "His research is still ongoing. But so far, he's found Adria has no criminal record, no known criminal associates, and has never filed for bankruptcy. I would never have offered her the lease to Falconer Lodge if she were an ex-con."

Elaine stroked her chin. "I suppose no news is good news. Now we can go ahead with crafting a strategy to tell the label and your fans that you're a father."

"I'll need to talk with my pastor and brothers about that," Levi said. Elaine might be a PR genius, but Levi wasn't going to make any firm decisions without getting input from Noah, Ezra, and Zach. "It's got to be handled right...for Owen's sake."

# Chapter 14

Adria scrubbed hard at the kitchen sink, even though she knew the rust-colored stains would never be completely gone. So much of the grottiness and dinginess of this apartment was beyond the power of elbow grease. Goodness knows she'd tried to remove it for over two years. Still, she was determined to leave the place spotless.

Most of her belongings were already on the way to the Falconers' estate, ferried by the moving company Levi had hired. He was covering all the moving costs, as if he wasn't giving her enough already.

The doorbell rang, and Adria blew a lock of hair off her sweat-beaded forehead. It couldn't be her ride to Surrey. She wasn't supposed to be picked up for another hour.

She opened the door to a beaming Katie.

"Hi, sweetheart," her friend said, giving her a hug. "Owen's down for his nap and Mum's in the house, so I thought I'd pop round and help with whatever else needs doing."

She glanced around Adria's empty apartment. "Wow, you've been busy. What can I do?"

"I've still got the windows and mirrors to clean." Adria handed her a rag and a bottle of window cleaner. "Thanks so much. I could use the help."

Katie spritzed the living room window—the same one Mike's cronies had smashed with a brick. "I'm thrilled you're getting out of this place. You're beating me by two weeks."

"I never thought I'd say this, but part of me is a bit sad to go." Adria wiped Owen's finger marks off a pane of glass.

Katie threw her a look. "Really? What will you miss most? The mold, the drug paraphernalia in the playground, or the police having to break up drunken brawls every weekend? Or perhaps Mike?"

Adria laughed. "When you put it like that, I'm well shot of this place."

"You are indeed. Leave, and never look back."

Adria paused in her window polishing. "I'll miss you, though."

"Now look what you've done. You've gone and made me cry." Katie half-laughed and half-sobbed.

"You're going to set me off too!" Adria wiped her eyes.

Fanning her face with her hands, Katie drew a deep breath. "I'm not going to have a proper cry until later. Right now, let's get the job done. Are you going to hand the keys over today?"

Adria shook her head. "I thought I'd hang on to them for a couple of weeks in case the new place is a total disaster."

"What?" Katie stared at Adria. "You need your head examined. What kind of disaster could you be expecting? How much worse could it be than this place? Owen's dad is being incredibly generous."

And that was the problem. He was giving her way too much.

She sighed. "I don't know. I only wanted a little help. If I let myself get used to Levi paying for everything, I might get the rug pulled from under me. Or if I become too dependent on him, I might have to go along with things I don't want."

Katie frowned. "Are you worried he might take advantage of you?"

"No, not in that way." Adria's face burned. "I mean... Forget it. Maybe I'm just too suspicious."

Katie rested a hand on her hip. "I kind of get what you're saying, but I'm struggling to get my head around the concept of too much money being a problem when it's getting you out of a paradise like this."

"You're right." Adria glanced at the empty room. Despite the deep cleaning, the odor of mildew still lingered. Her first priority was getting Owen out of this place. That was done. Next, she could focus on bettering herself so she could stand on her own two feet and support her son on her own if she ever needed to again. "Let's finish up here so I can get going."

Just as Adria wiped down the last window, her phone chirped with a text message.

She looked at Katie. "It's Phillip, the Falconers' driver. He's waiting in the parking lot to take Owen and me when we're ready."

Katie bit her lip. "So, it's time, then?"

"I guess." Adria looked around her. The apartment was pristine. Or, at least, as pristine as she could make it. She needed to gather her cleaning supplies, fetch Owen from Katie's place, and say goodbye to Meadow Hill. Hopefully, forever.

She put her rag and the window cleaner into a bucket. "I'll come over and get Owen."

"Oh, I nearly forgot." Katie reached into the back pocket of her cargo pants and pulled out an envelope. "Bella asked me to give you this. Mike checks her mobile phone, socials, and email, so she couldn't get in touch any other way."

Adria took the envelope and stared at her own name, written in green ink.

Katie picked up the bucket. "I'll take these to my place. See you in a minute?"

"Yeah."

As Katie left the apartment, Adria tore open the envelope and read the note.

Dear Adria,

> Katie says your moving to Surry to stay with Owens dad. She says he's not short of a bob or two. You deserve it. You were always kind to us.

I'll miss you. I know things haven't been right for awhile, but I'm still your frend and thinking about you allot.

Charlie and I are fine. No hard feelings about the social coming. Their just going to moniter us and give some support. Mikes not to bad if I don't menshun you.

Got to go but wanted to wish you well.

Xxx Bella

The final words of the note blurred as Adria wiped the tears away. She hoped her friend would see sense and dump that waste of space she called a boyfriend. Adria had done all she could.

Now it was time to start a new chapter in her own life.

# Chapter 15

ADRIA STARED OPEN-MOUTHED as the driver pulled up in front of the one-story house on the grounds of the Falconhurst estate. Was this where she and Owen would live?

It was postcard perfect. Pink rhododendrons were in full bloom in the front yard. A cobblestone path, bordered with tidy hedges, ran up to the dark blue front door. And she'd never seen grass this green. Would she have to maintain all of this? She didn't know the first thing about gardening.

The door opened and Beth Falconer stepped out, her face lighting up as Adria got out of the car. The older woman rushed forward, pulling Adria into a hug. "Welcome! It's so good to see you."

"Thanks," Adria said, warmth spreading through her at Beth's greeting. "It's great to be here. I'll just get Owen out."

She unbuckled him from his car seat, smiling as his wide-eyed gaze took everything in. "We've come to our new home, Owen. And look who's here. It's your nana."

Beth pressed a hand over her heart. "Nana! I love it."

She leaned closer to Owen. "Hello, darling. Did you have a long car ride?"

Owen lay his head on Adria's shoulder, giving his best impression of a shy child.

Her eyes shining, Beth turned to Adria, holding out a set of keys. "These are yours. Front door, back door, garden shed. The movers have already unloaded your things. Come on in."

Adria took the keys and followed Beth into the house. Large windows let in a flood of natural light which reflected off gleaming hardwood floors. It had clearly been decorated with the same taste and skilled hand as whoever had worked on the main house. And there was not a whiff of mold. Just the faintest trace of lemon.

Her beat-up chairs and coffee table were out of place among the other furniture in the elegant open plan living room, like a group of scruffy hobos surrounded by super models. Several boxes stood against the walls.

She put Owen down and he ran straight to the faded sofa, grinning as he clambered onto it. Perhaps it wouldn't be a bad thing having some familiar furniture around, at least for a while. She'd detested Meadow Hill, but it was the only home Owen had ever known.

Beth gestured around her. "This used to be the stables many years ago, but the previous owner made it into a guest house. There are two double bedrooms. One has an en suite bathroom, so that's where we put your bed. You labeled the boxes clearly, so the movers put everything in the rooms where they belonged. I hope that'll make unpacking a bit easier, although it's never a fun job, is it?"

Adria shook her head. "I'm not sure which is worse—packing or unpacking."

"Oh, I can relate," Beth said. "But I think packing is worse. Especially with a little one underfoot."

They both looked at Owen, who pulled books out of a box, leaving them scattered on the floor. That wouldn't do.

Adria scooped him up. She'd better find some of his toys to keep him busy while she unpacked.

Beth pointed toward a window. "There's a small, enclosed backyard, which I hope will give you some peace of mind. You won't have to worry about Owen wandering off. Our gardener maintains the outdoor space, but if you'd rather do it yourself, you're free to take over."

Adria shook her head emphatically. "No, absolutely not. I'm relieved to hear I don't have to do it. I've never grown anything in my life."

Beth smiled. "That makes two of us. I managed to kill a potted cactus plant once."

Adria chuckled.

Beth said, "If you like, I've got a free hour before I need to be somewhere else. I'm happy to help you settle in and get things in order."

"Are you sure?"

"It's not a problem at all. I'd love to lend a hand."

Staring into the older woman's kind blue eyes, Adria believed that the offer had come from Beth's heart.

Her defenses crumbled. "Thank you so much. To be honest, I wondered how much I'd be able to do before Owen's bedtime. And I need to grab a few groceries as well."

Beth gestured in the direction of the kitchen. "If it's any help, I took the liberty of getting a few basics for the kitchen and bathroom. I imagined you might be too exhausted to do a grocery run on top of everything else."

Beth's thoughtfulness touched Adria deeply. "I...I don't know what to say. I really appreciate that."

"Not at all. So, where shall we start?"

Adria looked around. The living room could stay as it was for now. "Maybe we could start in Owen's bedroom?"

"That's what I'd have done, too. I wonder—"

The ring of the doorbell stopped Beth mid-sentence.

Adria remained still for a moment before she remembered. This was her home now. She, not Beth, needed to answer the door.

Face heating, she put Owen down and headed to the front door. She pulled it open, and her heart gave a clumsy lurch.

Levi stood just beyond, holding a colorful plush ball. He nodded in greeting. "I heard you and Owen got here. I thought, um, if you don't mind, I could take him out to play for a little while. Get him out of your hair while you get settled. Would that be okay?"

# Chapter 16

Levi looked down at Adria as she stood framed in the doorway of Falconer Lodge. Even in sweatpants and a wrinkled t-shirt, with her hair slipping out of a haphazard ponytail, she was way too attractive for his health.

He watched her face as she worked through his suggestion that he take Owen outside to play. He shouldn't be noticing the tendrils of wayward brown curls framing her face, or the way her freckles danced across her delicately shaped nose. It was an equally dangerous idea to wonder whether her amber-colored skin was as soft as he remembered.

She turned back toward the hallway. "Owen, come and see who's here."

Her words snapped him back to sanity. He was here to see his son. Not to ogle Adria.

Owen trotted to the front door and stared up at him, his little body pressed tightly against Adria's leg.

Maybe this wasn't such a good idea. Although Levi had been thinking about this child constantly, staring at his picture every day, this was only the second time Owen was meeting him. And on that first afternoon they'd spent together, Adria had been there. Would the little boy even be willing to go with him, without his mother around?

Adria knelt until she was almost at eye level with Owen. "Sweetheart, Lev—I mean, your dad is going to take you outside for a little walk."

*Dad.* The word echoed in his heart with a deep, sweet resonance. Dad. He was going to have to get used to that. Grow into it.

Owen glanced up at him.

Adria said, "You can play in the garden. And, look, Daddy's got a ball."

"Ball," Owen repeated, his gaze settling onto the colorful object.

"Do you want to come?" Levi held out a hand, his heart turning to mush as Owen's little hand closed around his index finger.

"Bye, sweetheart," she said, waving at her child. She straightened, brushing a strand of hair off her forehead.

# HOME TOWN MELODY

"I'll bring him back in about an hour. Sooner if he wants," Levi said.

Adria nodded, her arms crossed. She stayed in the doorway as he led Owen away. Perhaps she waited in case the little boy wrenched his hand away and ran back to the house.

But Owen walked steadily down the cobblestone path.

Levi matched his pace to the toddler's shorter stride.

Owen pointed a stubby finger at the pink rhododendron bushes. "Bee."

Levi looked where he gestured. "You're right. It's a bumblebee."

He followed Owen to the bush.

The child leaned forward, his nose almost brushing the flowers, studying the bee as it buzzed from blossom to blossom.

Excitement swelled in Levi's chest. Owen was going to live here. Right here, where Levi could see him every day.

There was so much Levi wanted to teach him—how to play football, how to play tennis, how to fish. Maybe

Owen was musical, too. Levi had pictured himself being a dad in some vague, indeterminate future. But in those fuzzy imaginings, there had always been a wife to go along with the children.

He'd never expected to be a father like this, with a child sprung on him, having to negotiate visitation and child support.

But Owen was perfect.

Levi studied his features, searching once again for any trace of himself in the boy's face. All he saw was Adria in Owen's golden brown skin tone, in his beautiful brown eyes, and in his mop of chestnut curls. She had given Levi a child as stunning as she was.

The bee flitted off and Owen crouched on his haunches, staring at something on the ground. He didn't seem to be in any hurry to go anywhere.

What was he looking at anyway? Levi leaned forward. "Oh, that's a snail."

Owen glanced up at him and pointed at the snail.

"Yes, a snail. He's got his house on his back and he's moving really, really slowly."

Owen stared at the snail, following its creeping progress along the ground with complete fascination.

Levi had planned to take him down to the reservoir to look at the ducks. But at this rate, it might take forever. He'd best just take things at Owen's pace, which didn't seem to be much faster than the snail's.

When Owen's attention finally seemed to wane, Levi asked, "Shall we go to the backyard and play with the ball?"

"Ball," Owen said, standing.

Levi smiled. "Yes, let's play with the ball. Come on. Let's go to the backyard."

Owen gripped Levi's finger again, swelling his heart with warmth.

They walked around to the back of the house slowly, with Owen wanting to inspect everything they passed— from the patterns of the paving stones to the bushes along the way.

Finally, they got to the backyard, and Owen let go of Levi's finger and ran onto the grass.

Levi held up the ball. "Shall I roll this to you so you can kick it?"

"Yeah."

Levi rolled the ball forward.

Owen made a desperate swing of his foot, but missed the ball by a mile. Losing his balance, he landed with a thump on his padded behind.

Levi took an anxious step toward the toddler, but the little boy's giggle proved he wasn't hurt.

Levi chuckled. "Okay, so maybe football's not your thing. I'm a bit rubbish at it, too, so I guess you take after your old man that way. Shall we try something else?"

Sitting down on the velvety grass, he held up the ball with both hands. "How about I roll it to you instead and then you can roll it back?"

Owen sat facing him, his legs spread out in a wide V. Clearly, he knew this game.

Levi said, "Okay, here we go."

He rolled the ball to Owen, who caught it in his little hands.

"Well done. Now roll it back to Daddy."

Owen pushed the ball toward him, and Levi cheered loudly as he caught it. "Yay. Now, to Owen."

Owen received the ball and rolled it back.

# HOME TOWN MELODY

"Daddy," Levi said, preparing to roll it again. "Now, to Owen. Brilliant. Roll it to Daddy. Thank you. And back to Owen."

Owen pushed the ball toward him. "Daddy," he said in his piping voice.

A glow spread outward from Levi's chest, thickening his throat and choking his voice. "That's right. Daddy. And back to...Owen."

"Daddy!"

The ball came rolling back to Levi. Hearing that precious, sweet voice say "Daddy" brought everything into focus. The shocking letter from Adria's solicitor and the paternity test had rocked his world to the core, spiraling it into a completely different trajectory. His life had changed in the blink of an eye.

"Kwirrel."

What? Levi looked at Owen, who pointed at the hedge.

"Kwirrel," Owen said again.

Levi saw a bushy tail disappear under the hedge. "Oh, a squirrel. That's right. We have lots of them here. Rabbits, too. And ducks."

"Kwirrel."

"He's gone. I think he went off to look for some nuts. Shall we go see if we can find him?"

"Yeah."

They stood, and Owen grabbed Levi's finger again.

He blinked back a sudden rush of tears. Scary and uncertain as everything now was, being Owen's father was exactly what he wanted. And it was what mattered most in his new and strange world.

# Chapter 17

Adria rested her forehead on the door, fighting an impulse to run after Levi and bring Owen back in. She was being ridiculous. They were just going on a short walk around the house. And it wasn't the first time she'd left Owen in someone's care.

But that someone had been Katie, her best friend, whom she knew inside out. Levi might be his father, but he was a stranger to her and to Owen.

And yet this was why she'd agreed to move here in the first place—so that Owen could get to know his father. She had to get a grip and get used to the idea of Owen building a relationship with someone she didn't know. Or even like. This was all about her son getting what he needed. And that meant his father being part of his life.

"Are you all right, Adria?"

She turned around, finding Beth looking at her, head tilted to one side.

Adria gave herself a mental shake. "I'm fine. So, shall we get started with the unpacking?"

"I'm yours to command."

They went to the bedroom where the movers had brought Owen's high-sided toddler bed. The room was painted a pale yellow. Sunlight streamed through the window, which looked out onto a lush backyard.

Several boxes stood pushed against the wall. Adria found where she'd packed Owen's bedclothes and handed the duvet and bedsheets to Beth.

"We had only one bedroom before. Owen's going to have to get used to being in his own room." She made a face. "Or maybe I should say I'm going to have to get used to being in *my* own room."

Beth laughed. "I can relate. With each of my boys, I always found it so hard to move the crib out of our room. And every time, I think they were ready long before I was." She smoothed the dinosaur-patterned duvet cover onto the bed, a gentle smile on her face. "It changes your life completely, doesn't it? Having a baby, I mean."

Adria smiled in response. "That's the understatement of the year."

From the minute he was born—long before, in fact—her whole life had revolved around Owen. Caring for him, working for his benefit, picking up after him. Now his world was expanding to include a father. And a grandmother.

Maybe that's why the sight of him going out with Levi had thrown her off balance. It brought home to her just how much their lives were changing. But it would all be good for Owen. It had to be better than Meadow Hill.

While Beth made the bed, Adria unpacked Owen's clothes and placed them into dresser drawers.

"Are you going to miss Essex?" Beth asked.

"I'll mainly miss my friend Katie, but she was moving anyway."

"That's the friend who babysat while you worked, right? Where's she moving to?"

Adria stared at her. "That's right. She's moving to Kent. I'm impressed that you remember."

"Well, thank you." Beth tugged a pillow into place. "And I assume you had to quit your job."

Adria nodded. Leaving had been bittersweet. Mostly sweet, though. "They were a decent bunch, and my boss said I can put him down as a reference, but I won't miss the night shift."

"Maybe you can find something here in Hatbrook. What kind of work experience do you have?"

Adria closed one dresser drawer and began filling another with Owen's t-shirts. "I've worked at a fast food place, obviously. Retail, call center..." She hesitated, heat rushing to her face. "Um, I've done housesitting. And I've done some cleaning jobs."

Beth nodded, pulling up a box and opening it. "What would you be most interested in doing? We know quite a few people locally, and I'd be happy to put in a good word for you."

"I'm not sure. I'll need to see what's out there." Her face heated even more. If Beth was talking about helping her get a job, she might as well lay her cards on the table. "I left school with no qualifications, so my job options are rather limited."

Beth's eyes widened. "Oh, I see."

Sensing the question behind Beth's words, Adria said, "My mum died when I was preparing for my GCSE exams."

"Preparing" was the loosest possible description of Adria's dazed dream-walking through school. With her mother being so unwell in the months before she died, Adria had already fallen hopelessly behind with her coursework. She'd found it impossible to concentrate on anything. Changing schools and foster homes in her national exams year hadn't helped.

Eyes filling with tears, Beth reached out and squeezed her arm. "Adria, I'm so sorry. I can't even imagine what it was like going through something like that so young. Levi wasn't much older than Owen when his father died, but at least he had me."

Something in Beth's voice stirred a place deep inside Adria. This woman actually cared. She wasn't just being polite. And Adria hadn't realized Levi had lost his dad at a young age.

"I'm sorry for your loss as well," Adria said.

"Thank you. We made it through by God's grace."

"It could have been worse for me as well," Adria said. "I was pretty lucky on the whole, although I wish I'd tried harder to at least get qualifications in maths and English. There are a few jobs I've tried for that won't even look at you unless you've got those."

Beth put a finger on her chin. "You know, I'm sure the last time I was in the library, I saw a flyer or something about programs for adults to get their GCSEs and other school qualifications."

"Really? I didn't know that was possible." After aging out of foster care, she was too focused on surviving to think about filling the gaps in her education.

"It absolutely is," Beth said. "If you're interested. Why don't I see what I can find out next time I'm there?"

Adria smiled. Just when she thought she couldn't like Beth even more. "I'm interested. Thank you." Looking around, Adria pronounced, "We seem to be done here. I should probably do the kitchen next."

"Okay," Beth said. "I'll need to leave in about twenty minutes, though. I have to attend Bible study this afternoon."

Of course. Levi and his brothers were in that Christian music group, so it made sense his family was religious. "Do you all go to church?"

"Yes, all of us are involved in our local church," Beth said. "How about you?"

Adria shook her head. The last time she'd been in church was at her mother's funeral. And before that, she hadn't gone very often.

Her last experience with a church had been more recent, though. When her friend Bella had had her baby, she'd wanted to christen him. But the priest or reverend pastor or whoever he was had refused, since Charlie was born out of wedlock and his parents still weren't married.

Adria had decided that Bella was well rid of a church that would turn a child away, blaming it for the circumstances of its birth and the marital status of its parents. Didn't the Bible say somewhere that Jesus wanted little children to come to him?

They went into the kitchen and Beth unpacked Adria's crockery while Adria put utensils away.

As they worked, Adria's thoughts kept tripping over Beth's comment about how religious her family was. Were all churches as judgmental as Bella's? Perhaps the one Levi and Beth went to had the same attitude.

Wait a minute. She froze, holding a whisk poised over a drawer. If Levi went to a church like Bella's, wouldn't he face a lot of fallout when it came out that he had fathered a child out of wedlock? Maybe he'd made her sign the NDA to keep her mouth shut so that the story wouldn't come out at all.

That would also explain why Levi might have ghosted her. He might think of her as some sort of loose woman. The kind who slept with a guy on the first date. Or in her case, she hadn't even waited for a date.

Her grip tightened on the whisk. But he was just as guilty as she was. And if his church was like that, she wanted no part of it, and didn't want Owen to have any part of it, either. There was no way she'd let her son be rejected or stigmatized for something he couldn't help.

"Oh, look," Beth said, pointing toward the window. "Looks like Levi and Owen are back."

# Chapter 18

LEVI REACHED FOR ADRIA'S doorbell, relishing the weight of Owen's head on his shoulder and the child's warm breath against his neck.

Before he could ring, however, Adria opened the door. Her gaze homed in on Owen. "Is he asleep?"

"Yes." Levi stroked the back of Owen's head. "We went down to the reservoir to look at the ducks and he dozed off in my arms on our way back."

She crossed her arms. "It's not a great time for him to sleep, and he already had a nap earlier today. If he naps now, he's going to be up until midnight. I wish you hadn't let him doze off."

Levi's hackles rose. "What was I supposed to do? He was absolutely exhausted."

Adria stepped aside, and Levi walked past her.

Beth stood in the living room, watching but keeping quiet.

Adria sighed. "Fine. I'll let him sleep for fifteen minutes, and then I'll have to wake him up. Maybe that will help him feel less tired, but he'll still be ready to sleep at the right time."

"Where should I put him?"

She pointed down the hall. "We've set up the room on the right for him. His bed is already made."

Beth spoke as Levi walked past. "I'd better head on out or I'll be late for Bible study. I hope to see you soon, Adria."

Adria replied, in a tone completely different from the frosty one she'd just used with him, "Thank you so much for all your help. I wouldn't have been able to get anywhere near so much done."

"Any time at all. I mean that. Don't hesitate to ask." Beth smiled warmly at Adria. "Well, I'd better go. See you later at home, Levi."

Owen's bedroom was tidy and inviting, and had a high-sided toddler bed dressed with dinosaur print bedclothes.

# HOME TOWN MELODY

Levi laid his son on the bed and pulled the duvet over him, allowing his hand to linger on Owen's head. He stared at the toddler for a long moment, then moved back to the living room.

Adria was there alone, putting books into a short white bookcase that looked out of place among the tasteful decor of the house. There were other pieces of furniture that were equally jarring. These must be the things she'd brought with her.

"You've got a lot unpacked in such a short amount of time," he said.

She straightened a picture book. "There's still a lot to do, but Beth was a huge help. And so were the movers." Turning to face him, she said, "Um...I wanted to say thanks for hiring them. They made everything a lot easier. And thanks for letting us stay here."

"You're welcome." He took a step forward. "I hope you'll get settled soon. I want you to know that this is your home, no different than if you were renting a place in town. You can come and go as you please, and you can have people to visit you as long as you give their names to the security guards at the gates."

"Okay." She narrowed her eyes. "And what if I want overnight guests? Like, someone sleeping over?"

"Overnight guests?" Did she mean she wanted a man to stay over? The thought soured his gut. Why hadn't it occurred to him that she might be dating and want her male friend to spend the night? She was young and beautiful, and he and she certainly weren't together.

It was well within the realm of probability that she might be involved with someone. And if she were, she would likely want this guy to sleep over sometimes. After all, she had slept with him after they'd known each other for only a few hours.

It made sense, but he still didn't like it. At least she and Owen were living close enough now that he could keep an eye on any men who came and went. Naturally, all he wanted to do was monitor who might be spending time with his son. Her private life was otherwise none of his business.

Levi crossed his arms. "Like I said, as long as you clear it with the security guards, you're free to have guests. Including overnight ones."

"Thanks for confirming that," she said.

Did she already have a guy lined up to visit? His hands tightened into fists. He needed to let it go. She had her own life. The only thing they were to each other was co-parents of that sweet little boy now sleeping down the hall under his dinosaur duvet.

Levi forced his hands to relax. He needed to focus on being a father to Owen and not think of Adria as a desirable woman. "I'm going to head home now, but I wondered if you'd be okay with me taking Owen swimming tomorrow?"

Her eyes widened. "Owen can't swim. He's never even been to a pool."

"He hasn't?"

"No. I've taken him to the beach to get his feet wet, but that's all."

"I see," Levi said. "Well, I don't mind teaching him. Does he have any swimming gear?"

She shook her head.

"I'll grab something at the supermarket," he said. "What time should I pick him up?"

She frowned slightly in the way she did when she was thinking, as he was coming to learn. "I like him to take a nap between noon and two in the afternoon, so if you take him in the morning, you'd need to bear that in mind. And he should have his lunch just before his nap."

"Okay." Levi hadn't thought about any of these practicalities. He'd just pictured himself in the pool with Owen.

What should he give Owen for lunch? Mum would be there, and she'd know. Or perhaps the easiest thing would be to avoid this whole lunch and nap thing altogether. "Maybe I should get him after his nap?"

She stood, smoothing her t-shirt. "I think that's probably best. I'll have him ready at two. Where are you taking him? Somewhere in Hatbrook?"

"There's a pool up at the house."

She stared at him, her face reddening. "Oh. I didn't know that. That makes it simpler."

"See you at two tomorrow, then. I'll show myself out."

Levi stepped to the front door. He liked this ad hoc visitation arrangement so far. He planned on making up for all the time he'd lost with Owen, the time Adria had raised him on her own.

He paused, his hand on the doorknob. Had she really been on her own, though? He didn't want to think about another guy stepping into his place as a father figure to Owen.

And Owen had never been swimming? What was with that? What else had he missed out on?

He closed the front door behind himself and started the short walk back to his house. Now that Owen was in his life, he planned to make sure that his son lacked nothing. And that he was fully involved in raising Owen, no matter whom Adria dated.

# Chapter 19

*E*LAINE STARTED TALKING THE second Levi opened his front door.

"I wish you'd told me that Pastor Noah was going to make his big announcement today." Her heels clicked on the hardwood floor as she walked past him. "Why did he do that, anyway?"

Levi closed the door behind her. "I gave him permission. Let's go to the living room. Ezra and Zach are already here."

Elaine insisted on having this impromptu meeting after Noah had told the Sunday morning congregation about Levi becoming a father and stepping down from his leadership roles.

Walking into the living room, she nodded a greeting to Levi's brothers before she turned back to Levi. "As your publicist, I ought to have been informed that this announcement was coming instead of hearing it along with everyone else at church. Who knows who'll go out and post something online about all this before we've released the news publicly?"

Levi crossed his arms. He'd rarely seen Elaine this worked up. "I get where you're coming from, but I wasn't really thinking of it as a PR matter. I'm a Christian before everything else, and Grace Community is my church family. I need to come clean with them about having a son. Owen's living here now and I intend to be out and about with him. People in the community will wonder who he is, and I don't want the church being harmed by rumor and speculation."

Ezra spoke up. "I thought Noah handled the announcement really well."

"Me too," Zach said. "The church family needed to know this upfront instead of through the grapevine. I'm completely with Noah and Levi on this."

Elaine threw her hands up. "Fine. Anyway, it's done now. And it means the clock is ticking. We need to tell the record label, your sponsors, and fans about your son before someone from the church posts about it on social media or runs their mouths off somewhere else. The statement has to come out tonight. We need to maintain control of the narrative."

Elaine was right, but Levi wished she would stay away from phrases like "control the narrative."

"All right," he said. "Who should we tell first? The record label?"

"I think we should put out a statement to our fans," Ezra said. "Transparency and honesty have always been our key values. If we're open with them, it will show that you're taking responsibility."

Elaine pulled out her tablet and stylus. "There's a lot to say about going directly to the fans. It would galvanize your fan base and create even more loyalty. And we can also shape the narrative by giving them the exact context in which all of this happened. I like that."

Zach held up his hand. "Hang on a minute. Wouldn't it be more professional to speak to our record label and the people who are sponsoring the band before we tell the world? They're taking a significant professional and financial investment in us. And any controversial developments in Levi's life or in any of our personal lives might affect their bottom line."

Zach then looked around, catching everyone's gaze. "Put yourself in the label's shoes and imagine what it would be like if the first they hear of this is through a public social media message."

Levi nodded. "That's a good point."

Zach leaned forward. "You get what I'm saying? I think it would show more integrity if you approached our business associates first. At least give them a heads up before going public with this."

"That makes a lot of sense," Levi said. "Okay. You've convinced me, Zach. We'll release our statement first to the label and our sponsors."

Ezra rubbed his chin. "There will be fallout, though. You do realize that. This could mean that we might lose the record deal and sponsors might bail on us."

Levi's gut twisted. Just how many people had his thoughtless actions affected? He might derail his brothers' careers along with his. Who knew how many of his fans who looked up to him might feel disillusioned? Jesus talked about how terrible it was to cause young people to stumble in their faith. Levi had considered none of that when he gave in to his desires that night.

And it might all mean taking a financial hit, just when he'd committed himself to supporting Owen and Adria.

Zach met his gaze. "No matter what happens, we'll stand behind you in this, Levi. We know your heart and we know that you're doing your best to do the right thing."

"One hundred percent," Ezra said.

Tears stung Levi's eyes, and it was a moment before he mastered his voice. "Thanks. That means a lot."

Clearing his throat, he turned to Elaine. "Whatever statement we make, I want it to be crystal clear that while I regret my actions, I'm not ashamed of my son. Owen might come across this information down the line when he's old enough to understand it. And I don't ever want him to get the impression that I'm ashamed of him."

"Absolutely," Elaine said. "And now that we've agreed on the way forward, I suggest that we get straight to work and figure out what to say in those statements. Because they have to go out today at all costs."

Ezra nodded. "Okay. Let's get down to it."

# Chapter 20

Adria laughed as Owen pinched a piece off his lump of dough and popped it into his mouth.

"Sweetheart, if you eat all that dough, you'll have nothing left for your pizza. Let's roll it out instead, okay?"

"Okay," Owen said, whacking the dough on the tray of his highchair with his tiny rolling pin.

The doorbell rang and Adria glanced down at herself. She was liberally dusted with flour—no state to have any company.

Wiping her hands on a kitchen towel, she made her way to the front door. Hopefully, it was just a delivery.

Elaine stood on the porch, looking as poised and perfect as Adria was awkward and messy.

Adria gripped the doorknob. What was she doing here?

Elaine's gaze ran from the top of Adria's head down to her ratty slippers, and back to her face. "I hope I haven't come at a bad time. I need to drop something off."

Adria crossed her arms. "Okay."

"It would be easier if I came in, because I need to give a bit of an explanation."

Adria moved aside so the other woman could walk in.

Elaine's gaze swept over the entryway and living room. "You've certainly had a lifestyle upgrade since the last time we met. Congratulations."

Adria followed her into the living room, glancing quickly at Owen in the kitchen.

The boy was still happily bashing the pizza dough on his tray.

Elaine snapped the locks on her briefcase and pulled out a white envelope. She held it out to Adria. "This is a credit card with a £1,000 limit. It has your name on it, but Levi will pay it off every month."

Adria stared at her. "I thought the arrangement was for the maintenance payments to be deposited into my account, not for me to get a credit card." £4,000 had been deposited into her account like clockwork for the past two months, leaving her balance healthier than it had ever been.

Elaine laced her fingers together, their nude lacquer gleaming in the light. "That's still happening, but this card is an additional perk in case you need to get something extra. For example, you could get yourself some new clothes from somewhere other than the bargain bin or do something about your hair and nails."

Heat crept up Adria's neck as Elaine gestured at her worn out, flour-caked sweatshirt and leggings.

Adria curled her hands into fists to hide her dough-encrusted fingers. Did Levi think she looked shabby?

Elaine got a sheet of paper and a pen out of her briefcase. "I'll need you to sign here, acknowledging receipt of the card."

Bending over the coffee table, Adria glanced at the document, found the place for her signature, and then scribbled her name on the dotted line.

Elaine took the paper and pen back and slid them into her briefcase, smirking as she closed it with a click. "You're a smart girl. If you want to keep the gravy train going, it would be wise to make yourself presentable, since you'll be associated with Levi through the child. I wouldn't advise going around looking like a bag lady."

A surge of rage washed over Adria. She'd had enough of this woman's attitude. Why had Levi sent her over, anyway? He could just as easily have given her the credit card himself. "There's no need to be rude."

Elaine's sculpted brows flew up. "I'm not being rude. I'm trying to be helpful. And now that I've started, I might as well make things crystal clear. Since your involvement with him, Levi's career is in jeopardy. Your financial wellbeing depends on his ability to earn an income. So, you need to do your part to minimize the damage you've caused. Levi wouldn't be in this situation if you hadn't gotten your hooks into him."

Heat flooded Adria's face. "There were no hooks involved. Levi is a grown man who made his own choices. The last time I checked, it took two people to make a baby. I didn't make Owen by myself."

"Yes, he made some unfortunate choices. And now he's paying the price," Elaine said.

"If you're done with what you came to deliver, I'd appreciate it if you got out of my home."

Elaine stood, the slap-worthy smirk still on her face. "Your home?"

"Yes. My home. One to which I reserve the right of entry. Get out and don't ever come back in here."

Elaine stood with infuriating poise. Her lips twisted. "You know, I'm glad the gloves are off. It's always nice to know exactly what I'm dealing with. Have a lovely day, Miss Baines."

*Have a lovely day, Miss Baines.* Sarcasm clanged in the woman's singsong tone, triggering a bell in Adria's mind. She had heard that voice before, saying those exact words.

She held up a hand. "Wait a second. You were the one I talked to on the phone when I left those messages for Levi."

Elaine froze for the span of a heartbeat, then scoffed. "I have no idea what you're talking about."

"It was you. You never told him I called, did you?"

"Like I said, Miss Baines, I don't know what you're talking about. I'm a highly trusted member of Levi's team. My job is to protect his interests from anyone who seeks to exploit him." Her gaze raked Adria from head to toe. "I take my role very seriously. Enjoy your new credit card." With slow and stately steps, Elaine made her way to the door and let herself out.

Adria stood with her fists clenched, fighting for control before she went back to Owen.

Was that woman speaking for Levi? If she was just his business associate, she wouldn't feel so free with her opinion unless he shared it. And if he held the same attitude Elaine did, it galled Adria to depend on him for the clothes on her back and the food on her table.

Levi should provide for his son—that was only fair. But she wasn't going to take handouts for herself any longer than she had to. Especially if they came with sneers and snide comments. The sooner she was able to pay her own way, the better.

# Chapter 21

"A DRIA! IT'S SO GOOD to see you." Beth enveloped Adria in a hug that radiated warmth and delight. As welcoming and comforting as Elaine was abrasive and repellent, Levi's mother was the unexpected highlight of Adria's move to Falconer Lodge.

Beth sparked a sense of wellbeing Adria thought she'd lost forever when she'd buried her mother. And in the weeks since moving here, Adria felt completely comfortable bringing Owen to spend time with her. Just as comfortable as she'd felt when leaving him at Katie's.

Beth leaned forward and spoke to Owen. "Hello, sweetheart. Have you come to visit your nana?"

"Nana," Owen repeated.

"Aw, my heart can't take it!" Beth put a hand to her chest. "Yes, you're going to spend the day with Nana, unless she collapses from a complete cuteness overload. When did he start saying that?"

"Just now, I guess," Adria said with a laugh. "It feels like he's coming out with a new word every day. Shall I pick him up at four o'clock?"

Beth scooped Owen up. "Four is fine. I warn you, though, that if he keeps saying Nana, I won't be able to resist giving him whatever he wants. Ice cream for lunch and binge-watching *Bluey*. But if you've got a minute, I've got something for you. Come on in."

Beth was always giving her things, and Adria had stopped objecting. What would it be this time? A scarf like one Adria had admired in passing? A scented candle?

Adria followed Beth inside.

Beth spoke as she walked toward the lounge. "I was at the library yesterday and picked up everything they had on adult GCSEs and post-secondary school education options from our local college. I put it all there on the coffee table."

"I'm touched that you remembered." Adria went into the lounge, where a stack of leaflets lay just as described. She picked up the papers and paged through them.

Beth was right—it appeared she did have more than one route to get school-leaving qualifications. And that meant even more doors might open—a job, maybe even a career, and financial independence from Levi.

The TV was on, although muted. Adria glanced up, her heart jolting as Levi appeared on the screen, as though conjured out of her thoughts.

He was on some kind of talk show, judging from the set and the sofa he sat on, and the attractive woman who sat opposite him, an earnest expression on her face.

Adria turned to Beth. "Did you know Levi was on TV?"

Beth made a face. "Yes. I know the gist of what he'll be talking about. Do you want to watch?"

No use denying it. "Yes, please," Adria said.

Beth picked up the remote control and hit the unmute button. "I'll take Owen to the backyard. Levi set up a little sand pit for him."

Adria stared at the gorgeous blonde TV host who leaned forward and spoke into the camera with practiced sincerity.

"Welcome back to *Faith Pulse*. I'm your host, Janet Donovan. The Christian music world is abuzz over the news that Levi Falconer, chart-topping recording artist and a member of the Falconer Brothers, fathered a child out of wedlock."

Adria's heart hammered faster. Levi had gone public about Owen?

Janet continued speaking to the camera. "The much-anticipated Falconer Brothers reunion album release is now on hold and one of Levi's biggest sponsors has dropped him from his spokesperson role."

Janet fingered her earpiece. "And news is just breaking that a movie deal that was in the works with Faith Films is also on ice following the news. Levi is with us today in the studio to answer all our questions in an exclusive interview."

The host turned to Levi. "So, Levi, first of all, you're a dad, but as far as we know, you're not married. You've taken a strong and vocal stand in the past for sexual abstinence outside of marriage. How did it come to this?"

The camera zoomed in on Levi's face as he cleared his throat. "Yes, I've been outspoken about how physical intimacy is sacred between a couple who have committed to each other in marriage. I still believe that."

"But you're sitting here having fathered a child out of wedlock. How do you square that with your beliefs?"

Levi held Janet's gaze, but his voice trembled with emotion. "My beliefs haven't changed, even though I failed to live up to them. I went through a rough patch and made the wrong choice to use a physical encounter to try to numb the pain I was in."

Adria sat down slowly. So, that's how he felt about their night together. She was just a convenient outlet which he now regretted using. Good to know where she stood.

Levi looked down, blinking rapidly, and the camera zoomed even closer as he swiped his fingers across his eyes.

"Does that make you feel any differently about people who may have chosen to have intimate relationships outside of marriage?" Janet asked.

Levi's gaze locked on Janet's. "I've never condemned or been judgmental about people who do that. But I have pointed out that it's not ideal. I believe God's plan is much better for stable relationships, but I don't deny that it's a very high standard to walk, and we can only do it by His grace."

"Some people have pointed out that it's taken you over two years to go public." Janet narrowed her eyes. "Why did you keep this quiet for so long?"

Levi swallowed. "That was my second huge mistake. As soon as I had the...encounter, I tried to forget it and sweep it under the rug. That was wrong. But I recently learned that I fathered a little boy."

"That must have been a shock," Janet said.

"It was." Levi held up a hand. "But I want to make one thing crystal clear. Although I'm not proud of my one-night stand, I *am* grateful to have been blessed with a wonderful child. He's completely innocent in all of this, and I'm determined to be the best father I can be. That's my top priority. Learning about him forced me to be accountable for my actions, which is something I'm working with my pastor about. I'm sorry for letting my sponsors down, but I understand their decision. I'm also sorry for letting down my fans who look up to me when I've used my platform to speak about the values of keeping our sexual expression within the boundaries of marriage. I haven't lived up to those standards, and I deeply regret that."

Adria didn't know how to feel. Had she somehow ensnared Levi that night? Made him go against his religion?

Janet said, "How are you getting on with being a father, on top of your career upheaval and everything else?"

For the first time in the interview, Levi smiled. "My son is amazing, and I'm learning as I go. I have to give credit to his mother. She's done a fantastic job raising him alone before I came into the picture, and she's made co-parenting a smooth experience."

An electric tingle swept over Adria's face. Wow. Did he mean what he was saying, or were his words just for the camera?

"What can you tell us about your child's mother?" Janet asked.

Adria's heart hammered in her ears.

Levi shook his head. "She didn't ask for any of this, and I want to respect her privacy. All I'll say is that I'm confident she's always put our son's needs first. Both of us know the circumstances aren't ideal, but we're doing our best to give our child everything he needs."

A shiver coursed down Adria's spine as his words filled the room. Maybe he was just saying those kind things because it played well for the TV audience. But for just a moment, she wanted to believe that he really had this high opinion of her and wrap his compliments around her like a warm blanket.

"That's a bright spot, at least," the host said. "Co-parenting is always easier when the other person only wants the best for the child. Let's talk about how this is impacting your career. I understand your new album release is on hold indefinitely."

Beth came back into the room. "I left my phone in here. Is that still going on?" She gestured at the screen.

Adria fumbled with the remote and hit the mute button. Her face felt hot from the glow of Levi's kind words about her. "I didn't realize how big a hit his career has taken because of…because of what happened. Are all the Christians going to turn their backs on him because of this?"

Beth's face clouded. "To be honest, I don't know. Many of us do like to point fingers. Levi didn't live up to the principles of his faith, but the truth is nobody can. That's why Christians are reliant on God's grace. All of us are."

Those people at Bella's church had certainly been the finger-pointing kind.

Adria said, "So, what happens when Christians mess up?"

"Well, first of all, we ask God to forgive us. And He always does if we're genuinely sorry. But sometimes, even though we are forgiven, there are consequences for our mistakes." Frowning, she put a finger on her chin. "I'll try to explain. Have you ever used a satnav, or a GPS, as some people call it?"

Adria stared at her. What was she getting at? "No. I don't drive."

"Well, I use my GPS a lot when I'm driving. I put in the address where I want to go and it'll tell me how to get to my destination. But sometimes my trip doesn't go as planned. I'll take an unexpected detour or make a wrong turn and get a bit lost, even if I have the instructions right in front of me. Then I'll find myself completely off the course I planned. But the amazing thing that happens is when you get lost, the GPS will create a new route, based on where you are now, and tell you how to get to your original destination. Am I making any sense?"

Adria frowned. "Kind of? A bit?"

"What I mean is, none of us planned this. You didn't and Levi didn't. But this is where we are now. And we all need to move forward, following God's direction for this new situation the best we know how. As far as I'm concerned, my life now has two enormous new blessings, even though they weren't planned—Owen and you."

Adria's eyes filled. Why did she feel so loved, even though Beth had just called her a wrong turn in Levi's life?

Beth leaned forward, taking both Adria's hands in hers. "It's a tough time and there are things to figure out, but I see so much to be thankful for. I'm sure Levi does, too."

"A GPS reset, huh?"

"Yup. Our destination is the same, but we need to figure out a new route to get there. God will show us all what to do, and that includes Levi's livelihood."

Adria squeezed Beth's hands back.

Beth said, "I'd better go see what Owen's up to. I left him in the sand pit."

She took a few steps toward the door and turned. "I know you were going back home, Adria, but if you're not busy, I'd love for you to stay and visit with me, too."

Adria smiled. "Thanks. I'd like that."

# Chapter 22

*T*HANK GOD FOR MUSIC, Levi thought, or else he'd never get any exercise. In time with the driving beat pulsing through his earbuds, his feet pounded on the path of the jogging route that took him around the family estate.

Blowing air through puffed cheeks, he came to the small, wooded area that his family called "the copse." The trees were a welcome relief from the unseasonably hot May sun.

The combination of music and exercise was perfect for keeping his mind off the state of his career. Elaine assured him that it was still too early to predict the fallout of his announcement about Owen.

But judging from the speed with which his sponsors had bailed on him, it was going to be a long, hard route back to doing what he loved.

There were some bright spots, though. He'd joined a small men's accountability group that Noah led. Even better, though, was his relationship with Owen.

Adria had been generous with visitation time, and he generally saw his son four or five times a week. Things with Owen had been going so well that he wanted to take the next step and have him for an overnight visit…if Adria agreed to that.

They limited their conversation to polite greetings and details relevant to handing Owen back and forth. But she seemed to be getting quite chummy with his mother.

He came out of the copse and onto a wide green field with a gazebo in the center. The gazebo wasn't on his running route, and he was going to pass by it on his way to the reservoir when something caught his eye.

Adria sat at the circular table inside the structure. He might as well ask her now about having Owen for an overnight visit.

He changed direction and headed toward her, slowing to a walk.

Her hair was piled on top of her head in its usual messy bun, and she slowly twined a stray curl around her finger as she bent forward, looking at something intently.

She glanced up as he approached, and he finally saw what she'd been looking at.

Several books lay open in front of her, covered with copious amounts of sticky notes.

"Hey. What's all this?"

"School stuff," she said.

His face must have been blank because she went on. "I'm trying to get my GCSEs in English and maths."

"Oh. Right. You don't have them?"

That was a dumb question. Why else would she be studying for a qualification?

She shook her head.

His P.I. had sent him a report on Adria, but there were limits to what he'd been able to find out about her background. Information about her childhood was particularly hard to get. But the list of menial jobs she'd held should have been a clue that she might have left school without the best grades.

There was still a lot he didn't know about her.

"Good for you," he said. "Is it difficult?"

"English isn't too bad, but I've had to get a maths tutor. I'm trying to get some study time in while Beth has Owen."

"I didn't see her at the house," Levi said. "Did they go out?"

"It was just a spur of the moment thing. She dropped in and said she wanted to take him to the soft play place."

"I see. Actually, I wanted to talk to you about Owen. I'd like to try keeping him overnight."

She blinked rapidly. "Overnight?"

"Yes, if you don't mind."

Her hand went up to the nape of her neck and began twisting that loose strand of hair again. "I don't know."

He stared at her. She'd been so generous with allowing him and Beth time with Owen that he hadn't really expected her to object. Or maybe that was it—were they asking too much and too often?

She looked up at him, shaking her head as though to clear it. "You know what? Fine. Yes, of course he can stay with you overnight."

"Are you sure? Because you didn't seem—"

"No, I'm sure. Sorry, I was just getting my head around the idea. He's stayed with my friend Katie while I was working overnight shifts, of course, but he's never not been there while I'm at home."

"I wouldn't want to push you to do something you weren't comfortable with," he said.

"I'll be okay with it. Really. It's really just a me thing and not an Owen thing. When are you hoping to have him spend the night?"

Levi winced. "I was going to ask for tomorrow, but perhaps that's too soon."

"No, tomorrow's fine. He's a pretty good sleeper, but he has a long bedtime routine and doesn't like to miss any steps. I'll write it all down for you."

She pulled her notebook to herself and turned a fresh page.

He watched as she wrote, drawn in by the soft contours of her profile.

He dragged his gaze away to look at one of her books instead—*Understanding Maths: Geometry and Measurement*. Much safer to look at that. Was she really trying to get her GCSEs? Why hadn't she gotten them in the first place?

He paced around the gazebo, relishing the fresh breeze that kicked up and cooled down his skin.

"Here you go. I think that's everything."

He turned around and took the paper she held out. "Thanks. Wow, you weren't lying. It's a long routine, all right. But I'll make sure I stick to every single step."

She fidgeted with her pen. "Hey, listen, I wanted to tell you that I saw your interview the other day on that talk show. Was it *Faith Heartbeat*?"

He stared at her. He knew exactly what Adria had watched. On Elaine's advice that an exclusive interview would be more impactful, he'd done just one talk show.

"*Faith Pulse* with Janet Donovan. You watched that?" His face heated as his mind flashed through the things he'd said. He'd had no problem baring his soul on national TV, but he felt strangely self-conscious at the thought that Adria had been watching.

She twisted her fingers together. "I didn't know...I mean, I didn't realize it would be so... I'm sorry your sponsors dropped you."

"Thanks. I appreciate that."

She looked at him. "Since your circumstances have changed, if you need to renegotiate the terms of the child maintenance agreement, I'll understand that. Owen and I can get by on a lot less than you're giving us."

"What?" Levi stared at her. She was worried that his income was dropping? "That's very thoughtful of you, but I'm committed to providing for Owen and will continue to do that. He's not going to pay for my mistakes."

She held his gaze for a long moment. "Well, I'm going to get my qualifications and start working so I can pay my own way. You shouldn't have to support me."

And yet...he did want to support her. She was raising his son. She'd done it without help for almost two years. It seemed only right that he should take on some of that burden and ease her worries about finances. Why did he feel like that? Was it his guilt speaking? Or something deeper?

He forced a joking tone into his voice. "In that case, I'll let you get on with your maths work so you can earn those qualifications. See you tomorrow."

# Chapter 23

LEVI SET DOWN HIS copy of *The Very Hungry Caterpillar* and glanced at his son's face. The boy had been struggling to keep his eyes open while Levi read, each blink lasting longer and longer as the caterpillar in the story chomped its way through heaps of food. Owen's eyes finally stayed closed when the caterpillar transformed into a butterfly.

According to Adria's handwritten instructions, Levi was supposed to read *Goodnight Moon* next and put Owen down between 7:30 and 8:00. It wasn't quite seven, but Owen's little body sagged with the weight of sleep, his head lolling on Levi's shoulder.

Levi made his mind up. "Come on, little man. Let's get you to bed."

He carried Owen into the room that Mum had designated as his bedroom. As soon as he'd told her Owen was going to sleep over, she'd gone into town and bought a bed that was shaped like a race car, along with lots of other fun decorations.

They'd spent last night putting the bed together and getting the room ready for Owen's first overnight visit.

Owen was too tired to appreciate their efforts, though. As soon as his head hit the pillow, he curled up on his side, pulling his Pikachu plush closer.

Levi pulled the duvet up and tucked it around Owen, letting his hand rest on the boy's curly head. "Shall we say a prayer? Father, thank You for a lovely day with Owen. Please help him sleep well and wake up refreshed tomorrow. Amen."

When Levi opened his eyes, Owen was breathing slowly and rhythmically.

Levi glanced at the owl-shaped clock on the little bedside table. It was only five minutes to seven, over half an hour before Adria said Owen should sleep. He would probably be up at four in the morning, instead of six. But the boy had clearly been exhausted. If he woke up at the crack of dawn, so be it.

Levi turned the ceiling light off, leaving a little night light burning on the table.

He walked into the lounge and groaned.

Toys lay scattered all over the floor, along with the Cheerios Owen had strewn everywhere. Who knew a small bowl could hold so many? The blanket fort they'd made was still standing, between two chairs and a long-handled broom commandeered for the purpose.

Levi cleared board books off his recliner and collapsed, stretching out his legs. He felt as wiped out as Owen.

Mum came in, her eyes sweeping the room. "Looks like someone's been having lots of fun."

"Yes, we have," Levi said. "I'll tidy up. I just need a moment to catch my breath. How do full-time parents do this every day?"

Mum smiled. "And you haven't even done everything that Adria would do on a typical day. You haven't cooked or done any laundry or cleaned. And you won't be working an overnight shift." She looked around. "He's already in bed?"

"Yes. She says his bedtime is 7:30, but he was tuckered out well before seven. I think he'd have happily gone down by 6:30, but I read him a story first."

"She's doing an amazing job with Owen, isn't she?" Mum said.

Levi couldn't argue with that.

Mum put her purse down. "I'll be around the next time you have him sleep over. I just thought it was important to give you some space today so that you could have a proper evening with him without me interfering."

"Well, please do interfere next time. I'm absolutely shattered."

Mum laughed. "I'll give you a hand tidying up."

"Thanks." He dragged himself to his feet. He couldn't let her do all the work. This was part of being a parent, after all.

He grabbed a handful of wooden blocks and dropped them into the toy box.

They worked quietly for several minutes before Mum threw him a look and spoke in a too casual voice. "You know, I got a letter from Greg today."

Levi's grip tightened around the wooden block he held. While collecting the mail, he'd seen the occasional letter to Mum in his stepfather's handwriting, with the unmistakable prison postmark. As far as he knew, she hadn't been to visit Greg, but he suspected that she replied to his letters. Why she chose to keep contact with that snake was beyond his understanding.

Levi heaved the toy block into the box with a crash, but remained silent.

"He enclosed this for you."

Levi turned toward Mum.

She held an envelope toward him.

Levi stared at it for a long moment, then took it from her.

Her shoulders relaxed and she blew out a sigh.

His name was formed in Greg's tight cursive with the blue ink of a cheap ballpoint pen. His stepfather clearly didn't have access to the black ink Montblanc fountain pens he preferred.

Greg had been obsessed with high end fountain pens. His stepsons used to chip in and get him one every Christmas. The last one they bought him cost over £1,500. Had Greg used that Meisterstück Blue Hour pen to forge Mum's signature when he'd signed himself the deed to Falconhurst?

Levi walked to the wastebasket. His gaze fixed on Mum's pale face, he ripped the envelope and whatever was inside into small pieces. The shredded paper fluttered into the bin.

"Tell him to stop writing to me. I don't understand how you still have any time for him after what he did."

"We're still married," she whispered.

Levi picked up a scrap of envelope that had fallen to the floor. "That's your choice. But he's dead to me. I want nothing to do with him. Ever."

"I know how badly he hurt you." Her voice trembled. "But if you hold onto your bitterness, it'll poison you from the inside and turn you into someone you won't even recognize."

"Thanks for the advice, but I'm not bitter. Let's talk about something else. He's taken up enough headspace."

He tossed the scrap of paper into the wastebasket along with the rest of Greg's trash.

# Chapter 24

Adria's heart thudded against her chest as the doorbell echoed through the hallway.

Levi stood on the doorstep, Owen nestled in his arms. "We're back," Levi said, a smile on his lips.

Owen held out his arms to her and Adria drew him close, kissing his forehead. "He feels a bit warm. How did it go?"

"We had a great time, although he wanted to go to bed a bit earlier than you said." Levi ruffled the boy's hair. "He crashed before seven o'clock and he slept until eight this morning. He might have kept going, but I had to wake him up because I have an appointment. Does he normally get that sleepy?"

"No," Adria said, frowning. Was he sick? "Maybe he's working on a new tooth or something. Did he eat breakfast?"

Levi looked sheepish. "I tried to give him some oatmeal, but he didn't want any, so all he had was half a cup of milk. I'd have offered him something else, but I have an appointment in fifteen minutes."

"That's all right. Sometimes it takes a bit of coaxing to get him to eat. I'll give him some breakfast now." It was Levi's first time staying with Owen for such a long block of time, so he didn't know all the ways to encourage the boy to eat. She'd had almost two years of practice.

"Thanks once again for letting me have him. We had a blast, and I hope we'll be able to do it again," Levi said.

"Of course. Say bye to Daddy, Owen."

Owen raised a hand. "Bye-bye, Daddy."

"Bye, little man," Levi leaned forward and kissed the child's forehead. "See you soon."

Adria took Owen into the kitchen and settled him into his highchair. "Daddy says you didn't eat your porridge. Do you want some toast?"

She put a slice of bread into the toaster and touched Owen's forehead again. He was really hot. Maybe she should give him some Calpol to reduce his fever.

When the toast popped out, she spread butter over it, then cut it into four triangles, just the way Owen liked it.

He picked one up and nibbled a corner, then pushed the plate away. He turned and pointed to the living room. "Car."

"You want to play with your cars? Okay."

Adria lifted him out of the highchair and put him on the floor.

Plopping down cross-legged, he pulled a couple of little cars from the toy box and pushed them around.

Adria dumped the leftovers into the food waste and turned around when she heard Owen whimpering.

The toast had come back with a vengeance, along with gobs of curdled milk, all over Owen's chest and the living room floor.

Adria rushed forward. "Oh no, sweetheart. Let's get you cleaned up."

She picked him up and took him to the bathroom. "I think I might need to take you to the doctor."

Balancing him on her hip, she turned on the tap to fill the large baby basin he still used. While the water ran, she picked up her phone and dialed the GP surgery. Thank goodness she'd registered Owen there straight after their move.

To her surprise, someone answered immediately.

"Hello?" she asked. "Is this Hatbrook GP surgery?" Adria broke off, realizing she was talking to a recorded voice.

She punched keys in response to a series of automated options, ending in off-key hold music. She remained on hold as she stripped Owen of his soiled clothes. He threw up again before she sat him in the tub, whimpering as he retched.

Finally, a human came on to the line. "Hatbrook GP surgery. How can I help?"

Adria moved the phone to her other ear. "I have an almost two-year-old who's been throwing up this morning. He's feeling really hot. Will the doctor see him?"

"Throwing up?" The receptionist then took Adria through a series of questions to confirm whom she was talking about, his date of birth, and his symptoms.

"All right, Miss Baines. The doctor will see him if you can bring him to the surgery within the hour. Is that okay?"

"Yes, thank you. See you soon."

She took Owen out of the bathtub and dressed him quickly in a clean nappy, sweatpants, and a t-shirt.

He retched again, but nothing came up. Probably because his stomach was empty.

She dialed a cab, not wanting to waste time going up to the main house to find out whether the Falconers' driver was free.

Adria wrestled the cranky toddler into his jacket, trying to avoid Owen's flailing limbs as he whined and squirmed. He burned with fever, his small face flushed a deep pink.

"I know, sweetie, I know," she murmured soothingly.

The cab pulled up in front of the house five minutes after she'd ordered it.

Owen started to cry in earnest, his wails rising in pitched irritation.

By the time they got to the GP's office, she was ready to wail right alongside Owen. She cradled him against her chest as they went into the surgery.

Several patients waited in the dingy reception area when they arrived. An old man hacked wetly into a handkerchief while a frazzled young mother tried in vain to quiet her squalling newborn.

At least Owen wasn't the only noisy child. But he was inconsolable, his face screwed up and splotchy. Nothing she tried worked.

Owen's name flashed on the queuing screen, directing them to go to Examination Room Two.

The doctor, a woman with graying hair scraped back from her face into a severe bun, looked up as they entered. "What's all this fuss about, then? Feeling poorly, are we?"

"He's been feverish and has thrown up twice. His dad says he went to bed early last night and woke up very late, and he's not eaten much."

"I see."

Despite Owen's crying and refusal to cooperate, the doctor took his temperature and looked into his eyes, then pressed her fingers gently along his jawline.

Finally, as the little boy buried his face into Adria's shoulder, the doctor said, "Seems like it might be a regular case of norovirus, very common with two-year-olds. Just keep him comfortable and hydrated, and you can give him some Calpol to bring the fever down."

"But what if he doesn't eat anything?" Adria asked. "He keeps throwing everything up."

The doctor turned to her computer and tapped a few keys. "Just keep trying with water and clear broth. No juice or fizzy drinks. It should pass within a couple of days."

"But the last meal he ate was dinner last night. And he's thrown up twice already. His father said he slept for thirteen hours, and even then, he had to wake him up." Adria felt like she was babbling.

The doctor leveled her gaze at Adria. "Is he your first child?"

"He's my only child."

"Mm." A lot of meaning was packed into that monosyllable. She gave Adria a long look. "I understand that you're worried, with Ollie being your only child."

"Owen."

"Sorry, Owen. First-time parents are often anxious, but we see a lot of norovirus cases in children his age. It should pass soon, especially if you do what I advised. Calpol, water, clear broth. If you're still worried, you can call the after-hours service."

The doctor was looking at the screen again.

Adria felt dismissed.

The GP was clearly done with her diagnosis.

Adria settled Owen onto her hip as she stood.

"Thanks," she said, and walked out of the exam room.

# Chapter 25

Levi walked up to Adria's front door, holding Owen's stuffed Pikachu. He'd forgotten to bring it with Owen that morning and was surprised Adria hadn't called or texted to ask him or Mum for it, considering how attached Owen had become to the toy.

He rang the doorbell and Adria opened the door a moment later. With her phone pressed against her ear, she raised a finger to Levi, motioning for him to hold on as she stepped aside to let him in.

"Yes, the GP saw him this morning," she said into the phone. "She thinks he has a viral infection and told me to give him Calpol to bring down his fever, but that didn't help. I think he's much worse." Adria paced up and down across the living room floor, her body radiating tension.

Levi frowned. What was this? Was Owen sick? As the thought crossed his mind, he saw Owen curled up on the sofa under a blanket.

The child's eyes were half closed, and his face looked flushed.

Levi walked to the living room and knelt beside him. His forehead was very warm. What was going on? He glanced up at Adria.

She was still on the phone, her brows drawn together in a deep frown. "All right, I'll wait for a call back then. Thanks for your time."

"Is Owen unwell?" he asked.

She pushed her hair back off her forehead. "Yes. He didn't seem like himself when you dropped him off. You said he hadn't eaten much breakfast, and when I gave him some toast, he threw it up straight away. I took him to the GP, and she said she thought he had a norovirus infection, the kind that children his age often get. So I brought him home and gave him some Calpol, but he didn't seem to get any better."

A cold shiver snaked down Levi's spine. Was Owen sick because of something he'd done? The boy had clearly become unwell on his watch.

Adria walked to Owen and cupped his cheek. "He was burning up before, but now he feels really clammy. He's been tired and grumpy all day. I can barely keep him awake. I had trouble waking him up from his nap, and his nappy has been dry all day." Her voice shook as she spoke.

She looked at Levi. "I don't think we should wait for that call back. I want to take him to the ER right now."

Levi looked from Adria's face to Owen and back again. "I'll bring my car around."

In less than five minutes, Levi was pulling his car up in front of the house.

Adria stood outside the door, cradling Owen in her arms.

As soon as the car stopped, she pulled the back passenger door open and put him inside, strapping him into his car seat. "I'll sit back here with him if it's okay."

"Yes, of course."

The hospital was only a fifteen-minute drive away, but Levi struggled to stay within the speed limit. He glanced into the rearview mirror, trying to catch a glimpse of Adria and Owen.

She leaned over the boy, her hand on his forehead. "He's falling asleep again. I'm really scared." The tremor in her voice caused him to depress the gas pedal.

Despite his lead foot and a clear road, the drive to the hospital felt like it took hours.

As they pulled up to the ER, Levi spoke to Adria over his shoulder. "Take him in while I find a place to park. I'll see you in a few minutes."

"Okay." Holding Owen close, Adria rushed into the hospital.

Levi drove to the parking garage, breathing a prayer of thanks as he found a spot close to the exit.

He pulled the parking brake and an unfamiliar ringtone chimed from the back of the car. Adria must have left her phone behind. He reached into the back seat for the phone and glanced at the caller ID—NHS 111. This must be the callback Adria was expecting.

Levi hit the answer button.

"Hello?" the voice said. "May I speak to the parent or guardian of Owen Baines? This is a callback from the NHS 111 service."

"Yes, I'm his father."

"Hello, sir. I'm the duty nurse giving you a callback. After considering your son's symptoms, we advise you to take him to the emergency room as soon as possible."

Levi's heart raced. "Okay, thanks. We're here now."

"You're welcome. Wish you all the best."

Levi jammed his phone into his pocket and sprinted down the road toward the emergency room, his breath ragged and heavy. His heart pounded in his chest as he ran through the doors and swiftly scanned the room.

It was dotted with several patients seated on blue plastic chairs, but there was no sign of Adria or Owen.

He approached the reception desk, leaning forward as he tried to keep his breath under control. "I'm looking for a woman who just arrived with a toddler, a little boy, just under two years old."

The receptionist glanced up at him through the thick lenses of her glasses. "What's the patient's name, please?"

"His name is Owen Baines."

"And what's your relationship to him, sir?"

"I'm his father."

"All right, Mr. Baines. Let me just have a look."

Levi didn't have the mental space to correct her about his name. His hands formed tight fists at his sides and he clenched his jaw as she tapped and scrolled.

After a moment that stretched too long, she finally looked up. "Right, Owen Baines." Her face was unreadable as she met his gaze. "He's been taken up to the ICU, sir."

# Chapter 26

LEVI SAT IN THE private ICU room with Owen and Adria. Dawn was streaking the sky outside the window, but Adria had not moved from Owen's side from the moment they had let her sit next to him.

An oxygen mask covered the boy's little face and a tube ran into the bend of his elbow, secured by a pediatric arm board. The IV dripped life-saving antibiotics into his bloodstream, medicine that Levi prayed was winning against the septicemia that ravaged his son's body.

Adria held Owen's tiny hand in hers. Her face was a canvas of fear and exhaustion, painted in the dark circles under her red-rimmed eyes.

He'd tried to convince her to get some rest, but she wouldn't budge.

Levi's phone buzzed with a text message from Zach.

Any news? Everyone from church is praying.

Levi punched a reply.

**He's stable and resting. On strong antibiotics. Doc said if we'd come even an hour later, it might have been too late.**

Levi swallowed. If Adria hadn't insisted on bringing Owen to the ER... He refused to think of the consequences.

Zach's answer came back quickly.

**God is in control. Let us know of any news. Mum says to tell Adria she's praying.**

God was indeed in control. That was the only thing that helped Levi keep it together as he watched his son fight for his life. He was powerless to help, but that didn't matter. God was in charge, and all Levi had to do was trust in Him. But waiting and trusting was so difficult.

Levi put the phone back into his pocket and looked at Adria, hunched in her chair. She worried him nearly as much as Owen.

"Adria, the nurses set up that cot in the corner. Maybe you ought to get some sleep."

She didn't respond. He was about to repeat his suggestion when she finally spoke, her voice low and hoarse. "I should have seen it sooner."

"What do you mean?" Levi asked, stepping closer.

Her gaze remained fixed on Owen. "I know him better than anyone. When he was off this morning, I just…I didn't realize how serious it was until it was almost too late. How could I not have seen?"

Levi stared at her. Was she seriously blaming herself? Owen was alive because of her. "Adria, you did everything you could as soon as you realized. Remember what the doctor said? If we hadn't brought him in when we did—"

Her gaze snapped to his, tears brimming. "Exactly, Levi. If I had realized just an hour earlier, think how much better off he would be right now. If he doesn't make it, it's all on me."

Levi crouched beside her, touching her arm. "You can't think like that. You acted the moment you knew. Owen's strong and he's fighting, thanks to you. You're an incredible mother. Don't doubt that for a second."

She covered her face with her hands, her body shaking with sobs.

Levi's heart ached as if it would burst. He wrapped his arms around her, pulling her close. "If Owen didn't have you, he wouldn't be alive right now. You're the one whose gut feeling told you there was something wrong. And you're not alone in this anymore. I'm here now. My family, our friends at church—they're all praying for Owen. And God—He's watching over us. It's going to be all right."

He felt the need to believe the words as much as he needed her to believe them.

Her body relaxed as he stroked her hair.

He pulled back, his hands on her shoulders. "Try to get some rest now. Owen needs you to be strong, and you've been up almost twenty-four hours straight. Come on."

He stood, raising her up with him, and led her to the cot in the corner of the room.

She didn't resist.

He pulled aside the bedclothes and she lay down, curling into a fetal position. He draped the blanket over her, tucking it around her shoulders.

Her gaze found his. "Wake me up in a couple of hours?"

Levi nodded, but he had no intention of waking her until he absolutely had to. She was physically and emotionally spent whether she knew it or not, and he wasn't going to let her break down. Not on his watch.

Her eyes drifted shut and, judging by the slowing of her breaths, she was asleep within minutes.

He pulled up his chair, placing it between her and Owen, where he could watch over them both.

# Chapter 27

ADRIA STARTED AWAKE AT a touch on her shoulder.

The room was full of people.

Owen. What had happened to Owen?

She sat up, looking around frantically.

Levi stood next to her cot. He was the one who'd touched her shoulder. His fingers were still on her arm. "Adria, the doctor wants to speak to us."

Her heart raced as she stumbled to her feet. She caught a glimpse of her son, lying still on the bed, eyes closed, monitors beeping around him. "Has Owen—"

"Owen's okay. Let's listen to the doctor." Levi's arm went around her shoulders, steadying her.

A plump, middle-aged woman with short salt and pepper hair and dark brown skin, stepped forward, smiling. "Good morning, Ms. Baines. My name is Dr.

Kizza. I'm the ICU physician, and these are my team of nurses and respiratory therapists. I have some encouraging news to share with you today."

"We could use some good news," Levi said, squeezing Adria's shoulders.

"I'm glad to oblige," Dr. Kizza said. "After reviewing the latest test results and monitoring Owen's progress overnight, we're very pleased to see that his condition has improved significantly. We've been gradually lowering the oxygen concentration in his mask over the last few hours, and his oxygen saturation levels have remained stable with this reduced support. He's also been breathing well on his own. So I believe it's time to consider removing the oxygen mask and allowing him to breathe on room air."

Levi tensed. "Are you sure he's ready for that?"

Dr. Kizza turned to him. "Of course. We wouldn't be here if we didn't think he was ready. We'll start by gradually weaning him off the oxygen support while monitoring him very closely. I'm here every step of the way, so don't worry."

"All right," he said.

Dr. Kizza nodded at her team. They moved quickly, one of them tweaking the oxygen machine while another stepped forward to put her hands on Owen's mask.

Adria held her own breath as the nurse eased the mask off Owen's face. For the first time since yesterday afternoon, she could see his features clearly in the harsh fluorescent glow of the hospital lights.

Dr. Kizza stared at the monitor.

Apart from its gentle beeping, the room was silent.

Finally, a smile spread over the doctor's face. "His oxygen saturation levels are holding steady. He's breathing well on his own."

Adria's body sagged against Levi, and his arm held her tighter.

Dr. Kizza's smile broadened. "He's turned the corner. Congratulations."

"Thank God," Levi said, his voice husky.

Adria was too choked up to reply. She would never take a single of her child's breaths for granted again. Not when each one was a precious gift.

Owen was going to make it.

# Chapter 28

IN THE SMALL ADJOINING bathroom of his son's hospital room, Levi tossed a soiled diaper into the bin, a smile tugging at the corners of his mouth. Never had he been so overjoyed to deal with such a mess.

The nurse had assured him that a full nappy was a promising sign of Owen's recovery. Levi would gladly change a diaper every ten minutes if it meant witnessing tangible proof that his son was on the mend.

He washed his hands and stepped into Owen's room.

Adria had somehow contrived to settle their son on her lap without disturbing the IV line that trailed from his tiny arm.

Owen's head rested on her shoulder as he listened to her read *The Very Hungry Caterpillar*, absorbing every word as though he hadn't heard the story a hundred times before.

As Levi watched her cradling their son, a deep, soul-stirring chord resonated within him, striking an echo in his heart. She was so good with him. Completely attuned to his needs. He couldn't have chosen a better mother for his son.

Levi's phone rang and he stepped back toward the window to answer it.

It was Elaine.

"Hi, Levi."

It was jarring to hear her voice. The world she was part of now seemed so far away and frivolous. "Oh, hi. What's up?"

"You didn't respond to my email, so I'm just calling about today's podcast recording session. I was wondering whether you wanted to—"

"I won't make it," Levi said.

There was a sharp breath on the other side of the line. But when she spoke again, her voice was still calm and professional. "Not make it? Why? This is with the Greta Giles show. You know what a hugely important podcaster she is. I thought we talked about this and what it means for your publicity strategy."

"Owen's in the hospital."

"What? What's wrong?"

Levi glanced at his son. "He has septicemia. He was very ill. The doctors said they started treatment just in time, thanks to Adria's quick thinking."

"I see. How's he doing now?"

"He's out of danger, but they're still keeping him here for a while."

"I'm so relieved to hear that. I'm sure that will track very well with listeners and your fans, and probably also the record label when you tell them today at the podcast."

Levi pulled his phone away from his ear and stared at it.

Elaine lived and breathed her job, but this was ridiculous. Did the woman only see things through a public relations lens?

He put the phone back to his ear. "I said I'm not doing the podcast, and I'm certainly not going to exploit Owen's health to boost my image."

Elaine was silent for a long moment. "All right, I understand that. And I certainly didn't mean you should use your child's illness in that way. But this podcast is a hugely important opportunity. It was very difficult to get this interview. Isn't it possible to take even an hour?"

"I appreciate all the effort you put in to make this happen, but I'm not leaving Adria alone to go through all this. Ask Greta if she can reschedule, but I'm not coming today. It's out of the question."

"Fine, I'll see what I can do. Good luck with everything."

Putting his phone away, Levi glanced up to find Adria's gaze on him.

She looked away quickly, her face coloring.

Levi's phone rang again, and he sighed as he pulled it out. Elaine was relentless. He hit the answer button, only then seeing that it was Mum calling.

"Hello, sweetheart. I'm outside in the waiting room," she said.

"Outside here?" Levi said.

"Yes. I know guests aren't allowed to visit children in the ICU. But I brought a few things that I thought Adria and Owen might need. And I wanted to say hello as well."

"Okay, I'll be out in a minute." Levi turned to Adria. "It's Mum. She's in the waiting room outside and wants to say hello."

"She came? Aw, I'd love to say hi, but I don't think I can." Adria gestured at Owen's IV hookup.

"I'm sure she'll understand. I'll let her know."

He stepped out and met Mum in the waiting room, where she stood holding a huge card.

"The people at church wanted to send a bunch of balloons for Owen, but we were told they're not allowed in the ICU," she said. "So, everyone signed this card instead."

"They did? They must have scrunched their writing up really small."

She pulled Levi into a hug. "How's Owen doing?"

"He's a lot better. He's alert and taking an interest in things. The doctors said if everything goes as they hope, they'll move him to the regular pediatric ward this afternoon."

"Thank God," Mum said. "Everyone's been praying. And how's Adria holding up?"

"She's really tired, but otherwise okay. I'll try to convince her to go home and get some proper rest, but I'm not holding my breath."

Mum gave him a long look. "I'm glad you're taking care of her. We're the only family she has right now. I brought her a few things." She held up a carrier bag. "Just a few toiletries and things for her comfort and convenience. I'll let you get back to them now."

"Thanks for everything," Levi said, hugging her. Then he said his farewells and went back to Owen's room.

Adria's eyes widened as Levi held up the things Mum had brought.

"Mum sends her greetings," he said. "The things in the bag are from her, and the card is from the people at Grace Community Church."

She took the card, color blooming in her cheeks. "From your church? They know about...about Owen and me?"

"They do."

Adria read the card aloud. "Dear Adria, our thoughts are with you and little Owen. We're praying for a full recovery for him and strength and comfort for you.

With love in Christ, the people of Grace Community Church, Hatbrook." She looked up at Levi, her eyes glistening. "Wow."

Watching her glowing face as she held the card from the members of his church, he suddenly recognized the melody that was stirring within him.

She was growing into his heart, but he couldn't let that happen. Not when they didn't share the same foundation of faith. He was in trouble.

# Chapter 29

With her friend Katie on the line, Adria held her phone pressed to her ear as she gave Owen's hospital room one last look over to make sure she hadn't forgotten anything.

"I'm so relieved to hear Owen's fine now," Katie said.

"I can't even tell you." Adria looked down at Owen in his stroller, mercifully free from tubes and wires. "The doctor says he's made an incredibly quick recovery."

"Thank goodness for that," Katie said. "Children can bounce back in the most amazing way."

Levi walked into the room, holding Owen's discharge papers. "Are we ready to go?"

Adria nodded at him while still speaking to Katie. "We're about to leave now. I'll call later."

"All right, sweetheart. Talk to you soon," Katie said.

Adria slipped her phone into her purse. "Let's go. I can't wait to see this place in the rearview mirror."

He grinned at her. "Neither can I. After you."

She didn't know how she'd have made it through this time without Levi, especially that first night in the ICU when she wasn't sure whether Owen would pull through.

Warmth spread across her face as she remembered breaking down in front of Levi and the way he'd comforted her with such tenderness as she'd unraveled in his arms.

And then afterward, she'd overheard him telling Elaine he would not leave her alone at the hospital and attend whatever event Elaine wanted him to go to. Was it petty that she found that detail extra satisfying?

She knew he was just being kind to her out of a sense of obligation and duty. But what would it be like if they were a real family?

She stole a glance at him as he walked beside her, pushing Owen's stroller.

There was no point in daydreaming. No point in yearning for something more. They weren't a family.

They were parties to a child support agreement, and Levi was just holding up his end of the bargain.

His comforting embrace and sweet words had been impulsive, driven by their shared fear for Owen. Now that their child was healthy again, they would return to their parallel lives, only intersecting as they handed Owen back and forth.

When they were settled in Levi's vehicle, he eased the car out of the parking garage and navigated onto the street.

"You know, I was wondering," he said as he signaled to make a left turn, "Why 'Owen?' Why did you pick that name for him?"

His question took her off guard, and she stammered as she answered. "It's...it's kind of personal."

"Oh. I'm sorry. I didn't mean to pry." He returned his gaze to the road.

She swallowed. "No, I'm sorry. I don't mind telling you. When I was around thirteen, my best friend's parents were expecting a surprise baby. She was the youngest and they had thought they were done, but apparently they weren't. The whole family was so thrilled. And I got caught up in the excitement of it all as well. They adored the baby even before he was born.

"When he finally came along, he was the most loved and wanted and spoiled baby I had ever seen. He was such a little sweetheart and he had everyone wrapped around his finger from the second he was born. They called him Owen."

She hesitated a moment, putting into words feelings she had never expressed out loud. "When I found out I was expecting a boy, I wanted him to feel as loved and wanted as that other baby had been. And I liked the name Owen, so it just seemed to fit."

He blinked rapidly as he stared at the road. "Thanks for telling me."

"What would you have called him? I mean, if you'd known?" Adria asked.

Levi glanced at her. "You know, I never really thought about that." He turned his gaze back to the road. "We have a sort of family tradition of using Bible names. Zach, Ezra, Elizabeth, Levi. I suppose I might have continued that with something like Joshua or Eli. But Owen is perfect. Especially when you tell me why you picked it. I'd have named him that, too."

"Thanks," she said.

They drove the rest of the way in silence, but it felt like a warm, cozy blanket, as though they didn't need to say anything.

Soon enough, they pulled up to Falconer Lodge.

"Here we are," Levi said. "Welcome back home."

Beth burst out of the front door as they got out of the car. "Hi, you're here!" She rushed forward, pulling Adria into a long hug. "Thank God you're back."

Levi got Owen out of the car. "We'd probably better give him his lunch, and then it'll be naptime."

Beth threw a glance at him with a half-smile.

As they went into the living room, several voices called out. "Surprise! Welcome home, Owen."

Adria stood still, stunned, as she looked around.

Levi's brothers were there, along with an enormous banner that hung over the wall with the words, "Welcome home, Owen." The room was decorated with a profusion of helium balloons.

Owen grinned from ear to ear.

"Wow! Thank you. I wasn't expecting this," Adria said.

Beth hugged her again. "It's the least we could do. We're so glad you're back and that Owen is well."

Tears stung Adria's eyes. She tried so hard to convince herself that she was nothing more than a baby mama, not a genuine part of the family. And then they went and did something like this.

It wasn't so surprising that Beth would be here, but she was touched that Levi's brothers had taken the time and trouble to come.

Then she noticed Elaine standing in the corner, staring at her with a smirk on her face. There was the slap of reality she needed. Especially since she'd told the woman never to come into her home again. Elaine was a reminder of where Adria fit in this whole scenario.

Beth said, "I've put several casseroles in the fridge and the freezer, so you don't have to cook for the next few days."

Ezra stepped forward. "All right, everyone, let's be off so they can settle in." He turned to Adria. "We're very happy Owen's better."

Adria smiled. "Thanks so much for everything. And Owen loves balloons."

"Those were my idea," Zach said.

Ezra rolled his eyes. "There he goes taking all the credit. They were his idea, but I picked them out."

"And filled them up with hot air," Zach shot back.

They grinned at each other, and Adria got the sense that they often joked around like this.

"Come on, boys, let's go." Beth squeezed Adria's shoulder as she walked past. "I'll call you later."

As they filed out the front door, Elaine lingered, saying something to Levi that Adria didn't quite catch.

Levi nodded. "All right. Go up to the house, and I'll catch up with you in a couple of minutes."

Elaine followed the others out.

Levi set Owen down and the boy made a beeline for the largest balloon of the bunch.

"I'll get the rest of the stuff from the car, but I wanted to ask you something," Levi said.

Adria looked at him. "Okay."

"With everything that's happened and with all the paperwork that we had to fill in at the hospital, I realized something." He shifted from foot to foot, looking suddenly nervous. "Could you put me on Owen's birth certificate?"

Adria's answer came without hesitation. "Of course. Absolutely."

The smile that lit his face made her pulse stutter. She was just the mother of his child. Nothing else. Now, when would her heart get the memo?

# Chapter 30

LEVI'S STEPS FELT ALMOST buoyant as he crossed the threshold of his home, the familiar scent of cedar and lemon polish wrapping around him like a comforting embrace. The day's sunlight streamed through the open windows, casting playful shadows across the polished floors, and touching everything with a promise of new beginnings.

He still rode the high of his emotions from the hospital—Owen's recovery felt nothing short of miraculous. And the weight that lifted off his chest was palpable.

Now with Adria finally agreeing to add him to Owen's birth certificate, it seemed the tides of his life were turning. What a difference from the last time he'd been here.

As he shut the door behind himself, his gaze fell on a basket by the hall table filled with all the mail that had come for him during the anxious days spent by Owen's hospital bed.

Levi sifted through them, his fingers flipping through envelopes as he made his way to the living room.

But then he stopped. Among the letters was a small, cheap envelope, its surface marred by familiar handwriting—Greg's. A surge of bitterness twisted in his stomach. Even now, Greg's shadow loomed over the peace Levi was desperately trying to forge.

Hadn't Mum told Greg to stop writing to him? Of course she had. But since when had Greg respected her wishes, or anyone else's?

Levi knew without opening it what the contents would be—more of Greg's groveling, the insincere apologies dripping with desperation, pleas for forgiveness that Levi knew were as hollow as the man who penned them.

Greg, who had slithered into the Falconers' lives with a facade of charm, only to swindle them out of millions and betray their trust in every way possible.

A flash of anger heated Levi's face. As if Greg hadn't stolen enough from him already, he was here to stain the joy and relief of Owen's homecoming.

Levi crumpled the envelope in a fist. The paper crinkled sharply, the sound a tiny echo in the quiet hall. With a swift motion, he tossed it into the trash can, the small act feeling momentarily cathartic but doing little to erase the sting of betrayal.

As the balled-up envelope thudded in the waste bin, Levi's conscience pinged. The Bible said he should forgive those who had wronged him.

No. Levi crushed the idea as swiftly as he had the letter. Greg had done too much damage, caused too much hurt. He didn't deserve another second of Levi's thought.

# Chapter 31

On Sunday morning, Adria stood outside the door of Grace Community Church, Hatbrook, gathering every shred of courage before stepping inside. She could have asked Beth to give her and Owen a ride to church, but she couldn't stand the thought of everyone staring at her and knowing exactly who she was.

They were the people who had prayed for Owen while he was in the hospital, all of them taking the trouble to sign that lovely card. They'd prayed for her, too, even while knowing she was an unwed mother who had messed up Levi's career. And their God had heard and brought her son out of danger. It seemed only right to come here and thank Him.

As she stood, still hesitating, Owen fidgeted by her side.

A smiling woman at the door turned toward her, catching her gaze. "Welcome to Grace Community Church," the woman said, handing her a sheet of paper.

"Thank you," Adria said. Was that the appropriate churchy response?

"The service has already begun, but just grab a seat wherever you'd like. Right over there in the middle on the left is a good spot," the lady said. She turned her smile to Owen. "Hello, little guy. Welcome to church."

Adria stared. Was it customary to welcome the children as well?

She walked in the direction the woman had showed.

A song started and everyone got to their feet.

Adria didn't recognize the music. Although, to be fair, her repertoire of hymns only extended as far as the more common Christmas carols.

A small group of musicians stood on the front stage. Zach was one of the guitar players.

She didn't recognize any of the others. A brief scan at the backs of the congregation's heads didn't reveal where Beth and Levi were, if they were even here today.

She found an empty-ish row occupied only by a young woman.

The woman turned and smiled at her, with a little wave, her eyes lighting up even more when she saw Owen. "Hello. Does he want to play with my little girl?"

A girl about Owen's age sat on a woven rug in front of the woman's seat, busily engaged in coloring.

The woman bent toward her daughter. "Lily, here's someone for you to play with. Would you like to share your crayons?"

Lily raised her blue eyes to Owen and held out an orange crayon.

Owen plopped down, eagerly taking the crayon from her hand.

The woman smiled again. "I'm Mary."

"Adria."

After flashing another smile, Mary turned her gaze toward the front of the church where the lyrics of the song were projected onto a large screen. She joined in with the singing, slightly off key, but making up in enthusiasm what she lacked in technique.

Adria hummed along until she caught the chorus and sang hesitantly.

The song ended, and a young man wearing a suit and a buttoned-down shirt with no tie walked to the front of the congregation. "Hello, everyone. Welcome to all our regular worshipers and a special welcome to anyone who's here for the first time. My name is Noah Chaplin, and I'm the pastor of Grace Community Church, Hatbrook."

Adria stared at him. He looked nothing like her idea of a pastor. For one, he was young and didn't wear elaborate robes. And he spoke in plain, sincere English, not droning along as though he were bored by his own words.

Noah's gaze swept the room. "I'm going to speak to you today about how God is our Father. I realize that for many of us, the word 'father' doesn't bring up warm, fuzzy feelings. For some, the word 'father' might bring a sense of dread. Or anger. Or crushing disappointment. Or nothing at all. In an age where there are so many deadbeat dads, absent fathers, abusive fathers, imperfect fathers, or no fathers whatsoever, I'm going to talk about our perfect, eternal, unfailing Father. The one who loves us, provides for us, protects us, calls us by His name, understands us."

As Noah spoke, Adria felt as though the words were aimed directly at her. She felt the aching gap in her own life, the void where her father should have been. Her own dad had never been in the picture.

Did God really love her the way Noah said? Did He know her by name? She hung on to every word that Noah spoke, wanting to believe it, but scared that it was too good to be true. There must be some catch, some hole in what he was saying. How could it be possible?

As he ended his sermon, Noah said, "If you want to explore some of these questions a bit more deeply, I welcome you to sign up for our Christianity Explored course that's starting on Thursday evening, right here in the church hall. There should be a flyer with more information in the seat pocket in front of you. Bring all your questions, big and small. We'll start with a meal, then have a brief talk and a discussion afterwards. All are welcome, and we'll look forward to seeing you."

Adria picked up a flyer and slipped it into her purse.

# Chapter 32

LEVI STEPPED OFF THE bus, the crunch of gravel under his shoes echoing in the still, dead air. A rusted metal sign proclaimed "Welcome to Meadow Hill Estate" in faded letters.

He didn't want to examine the impulse that drew him to this rundown place. But he'd felt an irresistible pull to see where Adria had raised their son for the first years of his life, to somehow connect with that part of her story.

His private investigator's report painted a bleak picture of the housing development, describing it as a notorious pocket of poverty and social decay, even in a town known for its economic struggles. But seeing it with his own eyes was another matter entirely.

Levi wandered the potholed streets, his gaze roving from the weed-choked village green to the soiled mattresses and busted appliances strewn about like casualties of abandonment. A few tidy homes with well-tended gardens hinted at owners who still took pride in their homes. But they were overshadowed by properties with rusting junkers squatting in the driveways.

He tried to imagine the original hues the architects had chosen for this place when it was fresh and new, before neglect had rendered the color palette a dreary kaleidoscope of scabby browns, dirty grays, and rusted reds. The city's center he'd passed through was a ghost town of vacant storefronts and boarded windows, the only life coming from pawnshops, pubs, and fast food joints.

He slowed his pace outside a burger shop that boasted it was open all night. Was this where Adria had worked the night shift?

Rounding a corner, Levi found himself in a rundown playground, recognizing it from the address as the one near Adria and Owen's former home.

A defiant pile of dog poo sat congealing beside a sign admonishing owners to clean up after their pets.

With a cigarette dangling from her lips and her attention on her phone, a young mother pushed her daughter on one of the few functioning swings.

Had Owen ever come to this playground? His mind revolted at the thought of his son playing amid such squalor. Would Owen have grown up here if Adria hadn't sought Levi's help? Or would she have found a way out on her own?

Perhaps she'd only involved him out of desperation for child support, a strategy for her and Owen to escape this dismal place. Would he even know he had a son if her circumstances had been different?

The thought gnawed at him, causing a growing ache within his chest. Levi attempted to shove those troubling reflections aside as he turned to leave, only to freeze at a familiar voice calling his name.

"Levi?"

He swiveled slowly, tension gripping his muscles, his heart thumping erratically as his gaze landed on Adria standing just ahead.

# Chapter 33

As Adria's gaze locked onto Levi, she wondered if her eyes were deceiving her. His face mirrored her own shock, confirming his presence wasn't just a figment of her imagination.

Had he looked any less astonished, she might have believed he had materialized directly from her thoughts. Given how often she thought about him of late, it seemed plausible that her constant reflections could conjure him up, living and breathing, right before her.

What was he doing in Meadow Hill?

She walked up to him. "It *is* you. I thought I might need to get my eyes checked. You're the last person I expected to see around here."

He pushed a hand through his hair, his face turning a deeper shade of red. "I wanted to see the place where you...where Owen used to live."

"Oh." Why would he want to do that? He'd lived in Falconhurst all his life. Did even know that places like Meadow Hill existed?

"I wasn't expecting to find you here," he said. "Did you come to visit some friends?"

"No. I came by to hand my apartment keys over to the council housing team."

She'd been hanging onto her council tenancy all this time, only giving her notice after Owen got out of the hospital. That's when Falconer Lodge had started to feel like home.

Levi stood right where Owen had found that syringe on the day when she'd decided she had to leave Meadow Hill. The housing estate in all its dirty, ugly glory lay before him. Would he think any less of her now that he'd seen her old neighborhood?

If he was going to judge her by her roots, she wanted him to get the full picture. "I was going to have a quick look around the apartment before turning in my keys. Do you want to see our old flat?"

He appeared surprised by her offer. "Sure. If you don't mind."

She did mind. She felt vulnerable and exposed. Meadow Hill was a part of her life that had been filled with struggles and painful memories. But he'd come here to see it, and she'd give him an eyeful.

She led the way into the courtyard, her gut clenching as she recognized Mike and his group of hangers-on loitering around.

"Hey darling, haven't seen you around for a while," one of them called out.

She sensed Levi turning in that direction, but she gripped his arm. "Just ignore them. They're idiots."

"Oh, got a new man, have you? It's about time."

Another added his voice. "What's she like in the sack then, bruv? A few of us have been itching to find out."

Shame and anger bloomed in Adria's chest.

Levi's biceps tensed beneath her fingers.

"Oi, speak for yourself, bruv. I already know," shouted a hoarse voice she recognized as Mike's.

The rest guffawed loudly.

Levi made another move to turn around, but Adria squeezed his arm. "Levi, please don't."

"I can't let them talk to you like that."

"They sometimes carry knives," she whispered. "They're not worth the trouble. I'll never see them again after today."

Then they were at her apartment. Adria pushed her key into the lock and opened the door.

Levi followed her inside, red-faced and fists clenched. "Do you know those men?"

She closed the door behind herself. "They're just a bunch of bullies who think they run the estate. One of them dates a friend of mine. He used to beat her up, and I tried to get her to leave him. Since then, he and all his buddies like to give me a hard time."

"Can't the police do something about them?"

She shrugged. "The police have bigger fish to fry. Anyway, those guys aren't my problem anymore." She stretched out a hand. "So here we are."

The apartment was empty, as she had left it. The smell of mildew assailed her nose and a layer of dust had gathered on the surfaces.

Adria watched his face as they walked into the living room, catching his tightening jaw as his gaze took in the peeling wallpaper and the black mold that had spread, blooming into mushrooms in one ceiling corner.

"It's gotten a lot worse since we left," she said.

He turned to stare at her. "You mean you had this mold problem while you lived here?"

"All two years. It was an ongoing issue with the council. They said they were fixing it, but you know how it is sometimes."

He looked away, walking to the middle of the room, his hand churning in his hair.

She wished she could read his thoughts.

Finally, he faced her. Something about his expression made her stomach flutter.

"I...I'm glad you were able to leave this place," he said. "I'm just sorry it wasn't any sooner."

He broke eye contact and the air whooshed out of her lungs.

Turning toward the door, she noticed a bunch of letters on the floor, lying as though they'd been shoved through her letter box. She'd not seen them in her rush to get away from Mike's heckling.

# HOME TOWN MELODY

"These must have arrived before my change of address notification kicked in," she said, rifling through the handful of envelopes. Most of them were flyers, but one looked official.

She tore the letter open, her heart thumping as she read it.

# Chapter 34

LEVI STEPPED FORWARD AS Adria's hand flew over her mouth. "What is it? Is it bad news?"

She shook her head. "I don't know what to make of this. Here, you have a look."

He took the letter. It was a solicitor's letter on expensive headed stationery.

Dear Miss Baines,

I hope this letter finds you well.

My name is Ash Patel and I'm writing to you on behalf of my client, Cedric Fairbanks. It has come to our attention that you may be the granddaughter of Cedric Fairbanks. We have established that his late son, Adrian Fairbanks, was in a relationship with your mother, Julia Lynette Baines, whilst staying in England in 2002.

Documents Mr. Adrian Fairbanks left after his passing indicate he was aware that his relationship with your mother had resulted in a child whom she had named after him.

After conducting thorough research and investigation, we have located your address and are reaching out to you at the request of your grandfather. Our client has been searching for you for some time now, hoping to establish contact with you as his only living relative.

Please know that this correspondence is entirely voluntary, and there is no pressure or obligation for you to respond. Our client would be grateful for the chance to communicate with you and to learn more about your life.

If you would like to get in touch with our client, please respond to this letter using any of the above methods of communication. We will then pass on your communication to Mr. Fairbanks.

Whatever you decide, please know that Mr. Fairbanks holds you in his thoughts and wishes you all the best.

Warm regards, Ash Patel.

Levi's mouth went dry. He handed the letter back to Adria. "Did you know anything about this grandfather?"

"No. I've never heard of him." She paced back and forth, the letter clutched in her hand. "And he's been looking for me all this time."

Levi wasn't so sure. Was this Cedric Fairbanks truly who he claimed to be? If he was legitimate, what could he possibly want with Adria? And what about Owen? A knot coiled in his gut.

Adria was devouring the letter with her gaze. "There's more here about my father than I ever knew. I didn't even know I was named after him, or that he had passed away. It matches the little I do know—that they met while he was on vacation."

Levi watched the unguarded emotions playing across her face. What was she thinking?

She looked up at him. "I think I'll have to write back, just to find out more."

A ripple of unease grew within Levi. He wanted to keep her and Owen safe. He hadn't got them out of this awful neighborhood just to lose them to some sketchy character who claimed to be her grandfather.

He tried not to sound like a wet blanket. "I don't blame you for wanting to know, but you'll need to be cautious. We know nothing about this man."

"Of course. But this is so exciting!" She grinned, and his heart twisted.

"Look at the time," she said. "I need to return these keys before the council offices close."

Levi had nearly forgotten their original errand. "I left my car at a parking garage in town. After you drop off the keys, if you don't have anything else to do, I don't mind giving you a ride back home."

She flashed a smile. "Thank you. Let's go. I never want to see this place again."

# Chapter 35

ADRIA SLID INTO THE front passenger seat of Levi's Audi as he got behind the wheel. His cologne mingled with the new car smell, creating an intoxicating blend.

The cream leather seat caressed her skin, its coolness a welcome relief from the summer heat outside.

The engine hummed to life with a purr, and the air conditioning kicked in, enveloping Adria in a cool breeze.

A sigh of pleasure escaped her as she settled into her seat.

"Ah, that feels good," Levi said, leaning toward the AC vent and closing his eyes for a moment.

Her gaze drifted to his hands on the steering wheel. He had such well-shaped hands, big and manly and yet with long, sensitive fingers. Her face heated with the memory of what those hands felt like on her body.

Swallowing, she pulled her gaze away. Thoughts like that could lead to dangerous places.

Since attending the evening classes at Grace Community Church and becoming a Christian, she'd learned that physical intimacy was something God had designed to be enjoyed within marriage.

She'd had a couple of boyfriends in the past and had taken it for granted that things would get physical sooner or later. It was just something you did when you were attracted to someone, she'd thought. And that was why she'd been willing to sleep with Levi.

But now she understood that the act was more than just a physical thing. It created a deep spiritual and emotional bond, one that couldn't be ripped apart without creating scars. She understood how when she had sex with someone, she left a piece of herself behind. And why she always felt so hollow and used.

Levi had known it was wrong, which was why he'd felt ashamed after being with her. Could things have been different if she'd met him under different circumstances? He'd once found her attractive enough to desire her. Could that lead to something else, something pure?

She'd thought he was handsome when she'd first met him. Charming and funny, too. But now there was so much more. He was generous and thoughtful. And such a good father to her son. She sensed that Owen meant the world to him. If only—

But, no. That was another treacherous line of thought. There was no point exploring that deepening well of tenderness in her heart, dreaming of possibilities that were destined never to be.

She would focus on the here and now, on moving forward and raising her son now that Elmthorpe and Meadow Hill were firmly behind her.

Levi steered the car onto the dual carriageway.

Twisting her body toward the back window, she raised her hand and waved. "Goodbye, Elmthorpe. I could say I'll miss you, but I'd be lying."

Levi laughed.

She settled back into her seat. "To be fair, though, it wasn't all bad. We had some good times. Although I guess Owen won't remember living in Meadow Hill."

"Probably not," Levi said. "I don't have any memories from before I was about three or four."

So, Falconhurst would probably be the first home Owen remembered. She liked that thought.

"Did you grow up in Falconhurst?" she asked.

"We moved there when I was about four or five." He glanced at her. "We never thought we'd live there, you know."

"I didn't know that," she said.

He turned his attention back to the road. "Falconhurst has been in the Falconer family since the Georgian era, but we were just a minor branch of the family tree. Then my dad's great uncle died with no kids, and since all the closer relatives were already gone, he ended up leaving the place to Dad, and then Dad left it to Mum."

"And both your brothers moved away when they grew up?"

"We all did." His jaw tightened. "Mum remarried and lived there with my stepfather. I came back to stay with her when he went to prison."

She stared at him. "Oh. I didn't know. I'm sorry."

His knuckles were white, but his face had gone red.

Adria was bursting with questions, but this was clearly a sensitive topic. Beth's husband was in prison? She wanted to ask more, but it wasn't her place. And yet she couldn't exactly start talking about the weather now. What was she supposed to say?

Levi sighed. "It's not something we like to talk about, but I guess you should know. It's not a secret. He's in prison for fraud. He swindled all of us—my mother, me, and my brothers. Mum most of all. He was having an affair as well. We almost lost everything because of what he did."

His voice held a tremor she'd never heard before. He wasn't over this.

"Thank God I made an album that did very well and helped us keep Falconhurst," he said.

"Wow. I had no idea." Poor Beth. The thought of such a kind, loving woman being betrayed like that galled Adria. Of course, her husband must have used her own sweet nature against her. "How...how do you come back after something like that?"

"God's grace. Nothing else," Levi said. "Mum's been through a lot, first losing Dad and everything that happened with Greg. But her faith has carried her through. And lately, Owen has been such a delight. It makes her day every time she sees him." He threw her a glance. "Thanks for being so generous with him."

A surge of warmth flooded Adria. Beth had been so kind to her and Owen. "No thanks needed at all. Owen loves her. And...and so do I."

She felt flustered after the words slipped out.

The smile he gave her did nothing to calm her nerves. It stirred a flutter in her stomach, making her insides quiver like jelly.

He turned back to the road. "She thinks very highly of you, too."

"That means a lot." So, Levi and Beth talked about her? Did Levi share Beth's opinion?

He was silent for a moment as he merged onto the A12, then steered the car into the fast lane. "So, this grandfather of yours. That was quite a shock, wasn't it?"

"I know." She was glad to talk about something else. About a different type of hope.

Her hand slid toward her purse, where the solicitor's letter lay. "I had no idea he existed. I didn't think I had any family left."

"Your mother didn't have any relatives?"

She shook her head. "No one close. She had some cousins, but they live in Jamaica and she hadn't seen them since she was tiny. She grew up in foster care because her parents had substance abuse issues."

"That must have been tough."

"I'm sure it was," Adria said. "But she was tough, too. And kind. Beth reminds me a lot of her."

His eyebrows shot up. "Really?"

"Yes, really. Not physically, of course. But something about how they make you feel…I don't know…" She groped for the right word. "Seen. Like you matter and what you think is important."

"Mum does have that quality." He glanced at her. "I'd have liked to have met your mother. I think I'd have liked her."

His words went straight to her heart. She was trying so hard not to let herself build unfounded hopes about him. Why did he have to say things like that?

# Chapter 36

*T*HANKFULNESS FLOODED LEVI'S HEART as the June sun bathed him and the gazebo at Falconhurst in its warmth. It was the perfect day for Owen's second birthday, but the celebration felt like so much more than just a birthday party.

It was a tribute to Owen's recovery from septicemia, a celebration of his life, and a thanksgiving for his presence in Levi's world—a trifecta of joy and gratitude.

Levi and Adria had kept the party small, so there were only a few family members and close friends.

Pastor Noah had come, along with his wife Eden, who had her hands full with the face painting station. She was adding cat whiskers on the face of a little girl whom Levi had learned was the daughter of Adria's friend Katie.

Along with Katie, there was another friend Adria had made from Grace Community Church, who had come with her toddler daughter. The children ran around the velvety grass.

Besides face painting, Adria, Eden, and Mum had set up areas for different activities, including coloring, making paper crowns, and other simple crafts.

Ezra walked up to Levi, holding out a gift. "Sorry I'm late," he said.

"Thanks," Levi said, taking the brightly wrapped box. "I thought Martha would be here."

Ezra looked away. "She's extended her tour by another six weeks, so we won't see her for a while. It seems to be going really well."

Levi raised his eyebrows. "Oh. I suppose that's good news for her."

"Apparently, they can't get enough of her in South Korea." There was an edge in Ezra's voice that Levi couldn't pinpoint, but his brother's smile was wide and bright.

"I'll just go say hi to Mum and mingle," Ezra said as he walked away.

Levi added the present to the already stacked gift table.

Noah strolled up to him. "This birthday party looks like a sign that the co-parenting is going well. How is it?"

"Not bad, actually." Levi grinned at his pastor. "As it happens, we've got an appointment tomorrow with the Registrar of Births. Adria's adding me to Owen's birth certificate."

Noah's face lit up. "That's marvelous news."

As if by mutual agreement, they both turned toward Adria, who chatted with Mum.

Noah said, "You know, it's been wonderful to see how well Adria has been settling in at church. She's a regular now at Christianity Explored. I was so thrilled when she made a commitment to the Lord."

Levi swiveled to face Noah. "She did what?"

"You didn't know? Well, she did. And by all indications, she is maturing very quickly. She asks some very deep questions, and it's been a delight to watch her grow."

Adria had become a Christian. His joy about the news was mixed with the same guilt that tinged every area of his life. He ought to have told her more about his faith. But how could he when he'd been the worst possible example to her?

Noah gave Levi a long look. "Have you thought about becoming a real family? Especially now that you and Adria share the same faith?"

Levi's mouth went dry, and his heart beat faster. He'd spent so long squashing down any potential attraction to Adria, considering where it had led the day they met.

He turned back to Noah. "I don't know about that."

Noah shrugged. "Just saying. But of course, you can't force these things. We'll keep praying for you, as always." He patted Levi's arm and walked away.

Levi's heartbeat thudded in his ears. A real family. Could it happen?

His feet propelled him to where she stood, deep in conversation with his mother.

"Have you been in touch with him?" Mum asked her.

"Yes. The lawyer gave me his email address, and I wrote him. And he wrote back. He seems to be a really sweet guy. We want to arrange a time to FaceTime or Skype, but he lives in Australia, so we need to figure out the time difference and a day that would work for both of us. But I'm really excited."

Levi froze. They were talking about Adria's alleged long-lost grandfather.

Mum gave her a quick hug. "I'm so excited for you. Imagine finding out that you have a family."

Adria grinned. "I know."

Unease grew in the pit of Levi's stomach. He took a few steps away. So this grandfather guy was communicating with her? He pulled his phone out of his pocket and wrote a text message to his private investigator.

**Hi. I'll be sending new instructions soon. I'd like you to investigate a gentleman called Cedric Fairbanks from Brisbane, Australia.**

# Chapter 37

Adria glanced up as Levi came out of Owen's room. Having him here, tucking their son in, seemed so right, so natural. It was the perfect close to a beautiful day, allowing her to cherish the illusion of their little family for just a moment longer.

"He went out like a light," Levi said. "Probably exhausted after all that playtime with his friends. It was a lovely party, wasn't it?"

Adria smiled. "Thanks to Beth. She knew where to go for all the things we needed. I didn't have to lift a finger. I hope everyone had a good time."

"I'm sure they did."

Adria gestured in the direction of the kitchen. "I've got a pot of tea going, if you want some."

"I'd like that. Thanks." He went to the living room and sat on the sofa while Adria poured tea into two mugs.

Then she brought them over, along with two slices of birthday cake. "I noticed you didn't have any of this. It's delicious."

"No, I guess I was busy talking with Noah." He took a bite of cake and chewed it, then looked at her. "Noah told me you've been attending Christianity Explored classes."

Heat washed up her face. "I have."

"He also said you became a Christian."

The heat intensified. "Yes, I did." Why did she feel so shy about telling him this? Maybe it was because of the way they met. She felt like a hypocrite telling him she was a Christian now, when he had seen the very unchaste things she was capable of.

A smile spread over his face. "I'm really glad to hear that."

Her heart swelled. "Thank you."

"I need to go, but before I forget, I have something for you."

"Really? What?"

"Well, it's a Falconer thing." He reached into his pocket and pulled out a long rectangular package wrapped in silver and blue paper.

"My brothers and I have a tradition where we always give our mum a present on our birthdays. So, I thought I'd keep the tradition going with Owen. And since he's only two, I got this for you on his behalf. Happy Owen's birthday."

"Wow, that's such a beautiful thought. Thank you." Her heart filled with a delightful warmth that threatened to flow out into tears. She took the package from him.

"Go on, open it."

She tore the paper. It was a jewelry box. Opening it, she pulled out a beautiful necklace with a delicate butterfly pendant.

She gasped as she took it out. "It's gorgeous."

Levi said, "Based on his favorite book, I assumed that Owen loves butterflies. Or maybe he actually loves caterpillars, but I couldn't exactly give you that."

Adria laughed. "He's all about caterpillars. But I'm glad you got me this instead."

She opened the clasp but fidgeted for a while, struggling to fasten it around her neck.

"Let me help," Levi said.

He took the necklace, and the heat of his fingers scorched her skin as they brushed the nape of her neck. She drew in an involuntary breath.

His hand cupped her cheek, and she stared up at him, drowning in the intensity of his gaze.

His eyes seemed to darken. Desire pooled within her and she leaned forward, her eyes closing.

Then his hand was gone, and there was the thudding sound of feet hitting the floor.

Her eyes flew open.

He now stood across the room, his face red. "I'm sorry. That was a mistake. I shouldn't do that."

Shame blazed through her as he echoed the words he'd said that night in Cornwall.

His voice was hoarse. "It's not you, Adria. You did nothing wrong. It's just me. It's just that I don't want to make a mistake."

She nodded, blinking away at the tears that burned her eyes. Humiliation was going to shrivel her to a crisp. "It's okay. I understand."

"No, I don't think you do." He walked closer to her and sat beside her, taking both her hands in his.

Her mind whirled as she stared at his face.

"I've already failed you twice. I botched things so badly when we were in Cornwall when I didn't control myself," he said. "I shouldn't have slept with you, and I shouldn't have run off afterwards, just leaving you hanging. I'm so sorry. Can you forgive me for that?"

"Forgive you? Of course. I figured out that you left because you knew what we'd done was wrong."

"Thank you." He squeezed her hands. "You're all I think about. The room lights up when you walk in. I've been attracted to you for a long time, but because of what happened before, I didn't know whether or how to act on my feelings."

She swallowed, too afraid to let her heart believe her ears. "What are you saying?"

"I'm saying that I don't want to lose my self-control. But I want a relationship with you. That is, if you want that, too."

Her throat tightened as she finally understood what he was saying. "I do. I would like to do that." Her heart felt like it would burst.

His thumbs brushed over her knuckles, causing her to shiver. "My hope is that we might eventually be a real family—you, me, and Owen. But I want to let it unfold at the right pace for both of us."

"I was afraid you might hold my past against me." Her voice faltered. "That you might see me as...unworthy. Dirty."

"Adria, no." He pulled her into his arms, holding her so close that she felt the thudding of his heart. "That's not how I see you at all. Please don't ever think that. You're not just worthy, you're precious...in every way that matters. My mistakes are even bigger than yours, because I should have known better. But the past doesn't define us. It's what we build from here that counts."

She relaxed in his embrace, as his tender words soaked into her being, finally sweeping her doubts away. "I'm so happy," she whispered.

His lips brushed her forehead. "Me too. Let's take it one step at a time."

"You know what? I have an idea." His breath tickled her ear. "Tomorrow after our appointment at the registrar, maybe we could make a day of it. Go to the zoo or something. Or Polesden Lacey."

"That sounds wonderful," she said. Their first day out as a family.

He pulled back, his hands resting on her shoulders. "I'd better exercise some self-control and go now. I'll pick you up tomorrow and we'll drive down to the registry together."

"Okay. Good night."

As he slipped out the door, she sighed, giddy with joy. Was it possible that her dreams were actually coming true?

# Chapter 38

LEVI CLOSED ADRIA'S DOOR behind him and stepped into the driveway, his heart soaring. He, Adria, and Owen were going to have a future together. For the first time in years, he could look forward with hope instead of backward with regret.

He'd seen the confusion and hurt on her face when he'd held back from kissing her. The sweet, sensitive woman thought he saw her as impure or less than. His deplorable actions in Cornwall must have planted that seed in her mind.

But she'd understood his reasons and accepted his apology. Things were finally right between them, thank God.

He chuckled aloud into the evening air. That sly Pastor Noah, telling him Adria was a Christian and dropping those broad hints. It would be fun to let him know what had happened tonight.

Levi shoved his hands into his pockets as he walked toward the main house.

He and Adria had all the time in the world to get to know each other better, grow closer, and let their relationship blossom. It was so much more than he deserved.

His phone chimed. He pulled it out and saw that it was a text message from the P.I.

**I've heard your voicemail and I confirm that I will begin investigating Cedric Fairbanks straight away.**

He'd forgotten about Adria's alleged grandfather in Australia.

His mother's words echoed in his head, words spoken when he'd told her he was hiring a P.I. She'd been against it, worried about the invasion into Adria's life. But this was about protecting them, about ensuring that this man claiming to be Adria's grandfather was who he said he was.

Australia was half a world away, and the distance only added layers to his worry. What were Cedric Fairbanks' intentions toward Adria? For all they knew, he could be dangerous. Could he disrupt the life they were just starting to build?

Levi couldn't—and wouldn't—let that happen. He would keep Adria and Owen safe, no matter what it cost.

He pushed his mother's worry out of his mind. There was nothing wrong with seeking information. It was better than being blindsided, the way they'd all been with Greg. Information was power, power that Levi intended to use to protect his fledgling family.

# Chapter 39

ADRIA'S MIND BUZZED AFTER her almost kiss with Levi. Her emotions had been on a tumultuous ride—the thrill when she'd seen the desire in his eyes and then the complete humiliation when he'd pulled away. Going back to a soaring height when he'd held her in his arms, called her precious, and talked about building a future together.

She thanked God for all that had happened in the last few months and for the possibility of her, Owen, and Levi becoming a family. He was a wonderful father, and with all her heart she looked forward to adding his name to Owen's birth certificate. She ought to have done it before, but she was glad that it was something she could do for Levi now.

And the emotional rollercoaster wasn't over yet. She was going to talk to her grandfather tonight on Skype.

She turned on her laptop, tidying her hair as she waited anxiously for the app to boot up. She smiled as her fingers brushed over the necklace Levi had given her.

At 11 pm on the dot, the call came through. She answered it with shaking fingers.

Cedric Fairbanks' distinguished face, crowned with thick silver hair, appeared on the screen.

"Hi, Cedric, I'm not sure what to call you," she started, her voice catching.

His face creased into a smile. "Hello, darling. We'll figure all that out. I'm just glad we can finally talk." His voice was warm, filling the space between them.

"Me too," Adria half-sobbed. "How are you?"

"Oh, I'm fine. Tell me, what time is it over there?"

"It's just after 11 pm."

"That's incredible, isn't it? Well, it's your tomorrow here. It's, uh, seven in the morning. I can't believe I'm actually talking to you, Adria."

"I know." Her grandfather was real. Her heart swelled with a cocktail of emotions.

"I've been looking for you for a very long time, ever since I first heard about you."

"When was that?" she asked.

"Well, I suppose the first thing to say is your father and I never had the best relationship. While he was growing up, I was still trying to make my way in the world and I was taken up with the business. I wasn't the best husband I could have been. His mother and I split up when he was quite young, and I thought I could make up for my absence by throwing a lot of money at him. And that didn't turn out too well."

Cedric sighed. "He struggled to settle, but he always loved traveling. He wanted to see the world, and I think he saw pretty near most of it. He met your mother while he was in England. Then he continued on his travels and passed away in Hawaii. It was a surfing accident."

"Oh no," Adria said. "That must have been awful for you."

"It was. There was so much I never had the chance to say." Cedric was silent for a moment. "It took a while for his personal effects to make their way back to me. "And it took even longer for me to gather the courage and the will to go through them. And when I did, I found a picture of a lovely Black woman, and a letter to Adrian telling him he was a father and that she had named the little girl after him."

Adria sat up. "So, that's how you learned about me?"

"Yes. He traveled all over the world, but he kept that picture and letter with him. I'm not sure what steps Adrian had taken to reach out to your mother, to be honest. The fact that he held on to those things tells me he might have wanted to. But ever since I found out about you, I've been looking for you, Adria."

Adria's throat closed up. And she nodded, but couldn't answer.

Cedric went on. "I, or rather my investigators, eventually found out that your mother had passed away, but they couldn't locate you. Since obviously you were a minor, you'd gone into foster care and it was a challenge proving my relationship to you, because I don't believe paternity had even been established. But we kept on looking. And we're so glad that it finally led to a result, and I'm speaking to you now."

"It's amazing, isn't it?" Adria said. "And you're a great-grandfather, too, now."

He laughed. "Yes. I went looking for a granddaughter and found a great grandson as well. But what about you, Adria? What was your childhood like?"

Adria shrugged. "It was all right. Mum raised me on her own. If she had any relationships, she kept it quiet.

When I look back now, I realize that she probably first got her cancer when I was about six. But she beat it once, only it came back and she passed when I was fifteen. I went into care and, judging from some of the horror stories I've heard, I got off pretty easy."

Cedric said, "And when I heard about that, I couldn't believe it. All these years you were growing up in foster care, and I could have been there for you. All because I wasn't communicating with Adrian. And Adrian wasn't in touch with your mother. All of this could have been avoided. I could have known you right from when you were little."

Adria said, "Maybe, but they were telling us in church the other day that all things work out for good for those who love God. Even the hurtful things. And I'm in a really good place now."

"Sounds like a great church," he said. "I wish I'd learned some of those lessons when I was younger. Good for you, having it all figured out at your age."

They talked for a while longer, and Adria looked at the clock and blinked in surprise. "We've been talking for over two hours."

"Have we? Now, you see the danger of having a chatty old granddad who loves the sound of his own voice."

Adria laughed. "I would happily go on, but I've got a really busy day tomorrow and I'd better go to sleep."

"Of course," he said.

"We should arrange another time to talk. Maybe if we could figure out the time difference, we could even talk when Owen is awake and you can have a chance to see him."

"I'd like that," he said. "And we should also talk about you visiting me here in Australia. I've got a huge house with lots of space. It's been too long since little feet ran around it."

"That does sound like fun. It's definitely something I want to think about. Let's talk again soon."

"Let's do that. Goodbye, my dear."

As the screen went blank, Adria sat back, a sense of peace settling over her. Had she ever been this happy? She and Levi were dating and her grandfather was in her life. God was sending blessings faster than she could keep up. Despite the twists and turns, everything was unfolding just as it should.

# Chapter 40

Levi pushed Owen's stroller as he and Adria approached the office of the registrar of births.

It was located among a cluster of municipal offices within Hatbrook's public library.

As they crossed the lobby, a voice called out. "Excuse me, excuse me, sir, Levi Falconer?"

A woman, likely in her fifties, rushed toward him with an exuberant smile. She pressed a bejeweled hand over her heart. "Yes, you are Levi Falconer, as I live and breathe. My name's Ethel, and I'm a huge, huge fan."

Levi's face warmed as he smiled back. He still had fans? "Oh, wow. Hi, Ethel."

She squealed in delight. "I have a huge favor to ask if you don't mind. Could I take a selfie with you? My daughter absolutely loves you, and she'll be thrilled to see this. She'll never believe it."

"Yes, of course."

Adria moved to the side with the stroller, giving them space.

Ethel giggled, her hands slightly trembling as she pulled out her phone. "I can't believe this," she murmured, and quickly snapped a selfie with Levi. "Thank you so much. Take care."

"Thanks, and give my regards to your daughter," Levi replied, watching as Ethel walked away with a grin that lit up the room.

Adria nodded at Ethel's retreating figure, a glint in her eyes. "I can't take you anywhere with all these fans mobbing you."

Levi laughed.

The receptionist ushered them into an office where the registrar, a gray-haired man, greeted them with a warm smile.

"Welcome, welcome. I'm Giles Carpenter. According to my records, Miss Adria Baines is looking to re-register the birth of young Master Owen Baines. This is the Master Baines in question, is it?" He smiled at Owen, who stared back at him.

"Yes," Adria said.

Mr. Carpenter turned to Levi. "And this is the natural father who is adding his name to the birth registry. Is that right?"

"Yes," Levi said.

"All right, have a seat."

As Adria and Levi sat, the registrar shuffled through his papers.

"All right, I have here Form GRO 185. And I am to understand that the parents were not married, nor in a civil partnership at the time of the child's birth, and neither are you married nor in a civil partnership now. Correct?"

Levi nodded. "Yes, that's right."

"Very good, very good." Mr. Carpenter checked over his documents. "We have the paternity test that confirms Levi Falconer as the father. And I also see that a child support agreement is in place. And we have Owen's original birth certificate and the parental responsibility agreement." He peered at Adria over his glasses. "Am I to understand that you wish the child's name to be re-registered as Owen Baines Falconer?"

Adria spoke up. "Yes."

Warmth surged through Levi. He blinked away moisture in his eyes. He hadn't realized that Adria wanted Owen to share his surname.

His hand found hers and squeezed it.

Mr. Carpenter glanced at their hands. "And I take it you're both in agreement with that."

Levi grinned. "Yes, that's right."

The registrar shuffled his papers together. "All the documentation here appears to be in order. Can you please show me proof of identity, such as a passport or driver's license? Thank you, that will do. Now both of you just need to sign these declarations, consenting to the re-registration of your child's birth and acknowledging Mr. Falconer's paternity. If you don't mind, I'll just call in my secretary to witness the signing."

He went to his door and called out, "Mabel, would you mind coming in here for a minute to witness this?"

The lady from the reception walked in, smiled at both Adria and Levi, and stood close by as they both put their signatures on the documents.

Mr. Carpenter collected the paperwork. "And that's all I need from you. After I send all this in, we'll review the application and the supporting materials. And if your application is approved, Master Owen's birth certificate will be amended, including his natural father's details and his new name. You'll receive confirmation of that, and you can expect to receive the amended birth certificate in the post. I presume you will be wanting to get that, right?"

"Yes," Levi said.

Mr. Carpenter beamed at both of them. "Very well then. We are all done here. Congratulations to all of you."

They stood and shook hands, and Levi pushed Owen out of the office in his stroller.

Adria looked up at him, her eyes sparkling. "Well, that's it."

He grinned back at her. "That's it. I guess that means I'm officially Owen's dad."

# Chapter 41

*A*DRIA STRAPPED OWEN INTO his car seat, then settled into the passenger seat next to Levi. "I've never been to Polesden Lacey before."

Levi glanced at her. "You're in for a treat, then. We used to go there when I was young, since it's fairly close."

Those outings were some of his most precious memories, and it thrilled him that he would pass on those experiences to his son. And to share them with the woman with whom he hoped to build a future and a family.

He allowed his gaze to linger on her face as she buckled her seatbelt. The summer sun had deepened her brown skin and added an extra sprinkle of freckles across her nose and cheeks.

She turned to face him, her brown eyes shining. "I was so busy getting ready for the registry appointment that I didn't tell you. I had a video call with my grandfather last night."

The record scratch moment halted the violins in his head. "I forgot to ask about that. How did it go?"

Adria beamed. "It was wonderful. Just like I imagined. We talked for ages, and he filled me in on my father and what he was like growing up. He even mentioned that we might want to pay him a visit in Australia."

Levi didn't like the sound of that at all. "And what did you say to that? Did you agree?"

"I thought it was a lovely idea. He said he could travel to England, but he's in his eighties. It would be easier for Owen and me to go there rather than for him to come here."

Levi glanced at her. "Do you think it's wise for you to take Owen halfway around the world to meet a guy you never even knew existed until a couple of weeks ago?"

Adria stiffened. "I'm not planning on jumping on a plane tomorrow. Obviously, we'll take the time to get to know each other better."

"That's all I'm asking," Levi said. "I want to make sure you're both safe."

Adria's body relaxed, and she touched his hand as it rested on the steering wheel, her fingers warm and soft. "Thanks. I get that, and I appreciate that you're thinking about our safety."

She moved her hand away. "But he's my grandfather. The only family I have. He's the only connection to my dad. I want to know him before he's gone, too. Is that so crazy? I'll take any precaution you want, but I need to see him."

Levi gritted his teeth. What was he supposed to say to that? He sighed. "I understand. But let's not make any decisions yet. We can talk about it later when we've found out more about him."

His P.I. was already digging up information on Cedric Fairbanks, but Levi wasn't about to mention that.

"Here we are," Levi said as they drove through the gates of the Polesden Lacey estate.

He steered the car into the parking lot and slowed to a stop.

Adria twisted her body so she could see the back seat. "Owen's asleep. The car ride must have done it."

She turned back to face him. "Should we just wake him up and go in?"

"In a minute," he said, his gaze tracing the delicate curve of her cheek down to the rounded softness of her chin. His fingers followed of their own accord, brushing a stray curl behind her ear before cupping her flushed cheek. He searched her warm brown eyes, giving her time to pull away.

Her lips parted on a trembling indrawn breath, and her hand came up to rest against his thundering heart.

This time, he didn't hold back.

Leaning forward, he kissed her tenderly, savoring the delicious softness of her mouth and the sweetness of her response. Even as desire built within him, he gentled the kiss, allowing himself only the most sparing taste of her.

When they finally drew apart, he saw that her eyes had drifted shut, her dark lashes fanning across her cheeks.

He ran the pad of his thumb along the plump curve of her lower lip, watching her mouth quirk with a smile as she leaned into his touch. She had never looked more beautiful. In that moment, he realized just how deeply he was falling for this woman. He couldn't bear the thought of anyone taking her or Owen away from his life.

# Chapter 42

*L*EVI HADN'T SEEN ELAINE so thrilled in a long time. She was always happy when his business was looking up, and things had been dire for a while. But they were definitely on an upswing now.

But even as they met in his living room and she gave him a rundown of the latest metrics that measured his public image, his mind drifted back to Adria, the kiss they'd shared, and the bond that was deepening between them. None of Elaine's glowing PR reports could top that.

Her voice dragged his focus back to the present. "There's a ton of positive buzz on social media about you and your son, including on a lot of Christian-focused blogs and Facebook groups, and sales of your solo album and you and your brother's other albums appear to be holding steady, so that's fantastic news. And last, but not least, there's this."

She held up a printed screen grab from a blog post.

Levi stared at the picture. "That's the selfie that a lady took outside the registrar's office in Hatbrook. She went public with it?"

"That's right," Elaine said, grinning. "Apparently this fan posted this selfie on her personal blog and social media, and it got picked up by another Christian influencer and then another. It's gone viral now. Internet sleuths put two and two together, realizing that it was taken at the registrar's office and that there was a mystery woman and a child in the background. The Internet has concluded that this must be your child and his mother, and everyone loves it because it shows that you're doing the right thing by your son."

Levi hid a smile. Those Internet sleuths didn't know the half of it. He wanted to keep Adria and their growing relationship out of the spotlight while they found their footing. "I didn't do the selfie for publicity. I thought she was just a friendly fan and I was happy to do the tiniest thing for her. It cost me nothing."

Elaine grinned. "And that's what makes it so perfect. It's the best kind of publicity—feel-good, unplanned, genuine, word of mouth. I couldn't have planned it better myself. Absolutely brilliant. And I don't think it's a coincidence that the record label is now talking about a potential soft launch of your album next year when things have had a chance to calm down."

Levi smiled. "That is good news."

Elaine's answer was cut off as Levi's phone rang. He picked it up and glanced at the caller ID. It was his P.I. "Sorry, I need to take this. It's from that investigator I hired."

Elaine sat up straight. "Oh, really?"

"Hi, Levi here."

"Hello Mr. Falconer. I've emailed you my report on Cedric Fairbanks. Since you told me it was urgent, I'm just calling to give you a heads up."

"Thank you, I appreciate that. What did you find out? Is he legit?"

"Oh, he's very legit," the P.I. said. "More than legit. Cedric Fairbanks is one of the wealthiest entrepreneurs in Australia, and he's well respected in the business community. Not a whisper of scandal about him, apart from an ugly divorce decades ago. He made his money first in real estate and then invested in the mining industry, in agribusiness, and more recently in the technology sector. He's got an estimated worth of about $75 million. He lost his only son about fifteen years ago."

Levi's heart sank. He'd been half hoping that his P.I. would discover that Cedric Fairbanks was a scammer of some sort. At least then he would have had a reason to keep Owen and Adria away from him. "Thanks for putting in all that work."

"Not a problem, sir. I hope that sets your mind at ease. Goodbye."

Levi's mind was not at ease at all. Very far from at ease.

"Is something the matter? Did the P.I. find out something wrong?" Elaine asked.

Wrong? It depended on how you looked at it. He looked at Elaine. "No. He was just telling me what he found out about this grandfather of Adria's who just popped out of the woodwork. Apparently, he is seriously loaded. He lives in Australia and he wants Adria and Owen to visit him. They're his next of kin since he lost his only son."

Elaine's eyes widened and she was speechless for a few moments. "Are you sure this guy only wants them to visit? If he's wealthy and they're his only descendants, as you said, what if he wants them to start a new life in Australia? Do you have any custody arrangements in writing?"

Dread sat like a millstone in the pit of Levi's gut. "No, it's all verbal. We were playing it by ear."

"That could be tricky," Elaine said.

Levi sat up. "But I did recently get my name added to Owen's birth certificate."

"That's something at least," Elaine said. "I think it might be an idea to consult with your lawyer in case it's necessary to prevent Adria from taking Owen out of the country."

Levi stared at her. Elaine was right. This Cedric Fairbanks could easily get Owen and Adria to pack up everything and move to Australia. And where would that leave him?

His mind went back to his and Adria's kiss and all the promise it held. But that was all it was. Promises were easily forgotten when money was involved. His stepfather had proved that.

Could Levi really trust what Adria would do? The reason she had reached out to him in the first place was because she was stuck in that horrible housing estate and needed financial help. Would she have come to him at all if she'd known about Cedric Fairbanks?

And what would she do now?

He stood. "Sorry, Elaine, but I'll have to reschedule our meeting, unless there's anything urgent to go through. I need to speak with my solicitor."

# Chapter 43

THE POOL ECHOED WITH delighted shrieks and splashes as Levi watched his mother guide Owen through the shallow end.

Mum's face beamed with a radiant smile, her gray hair plastered against her head as she laughed and encouraged the squealing toddler. "That's my superstar swimmer," she said, scooping Owen into her arms to pepper his cheeks with kisses in the summer sunshine. "Your mummy will be over the moon to see how far you've come along. She's working hard, too, with her books, isn't she?"

It warmed Levi's heart to see how close his mother and Owen were becoming. He would never have imagined things being like this. He was grateful beyond words for the way she'd embraced both Owen and Adria, who was currently holed up with her GCSE work.

He grinned. He knew exactly how to make Mum's day even better.

"I've got a bit of news for you."

Mum glanced up at him. "What?"

"Adria and I are dating. Properly dating."

Mum gasped, her hand flying to her mouth. "Are you serious? That's absolutely wonderful. The best news I've heard in a long time. When did this happen?"

"We've been keeping things quiet and slow over the past few weeks. You're the first to know."

"Wow! God is so good." She pulled Owen closer and squeezed him, making him giggle and splash water on her face.

"This is exactly what I was praying would happen," she said. "I am so, so happy for you. She's such a lovely girl. And I'm so glad about how well things are turning out for her. She's become a Christian, and she's getting her studies on track, getting her qualifications. And now she's been put in contact with this long-lost grandfather of hers. God is so amazing. He's been answering every single one of my prayers for her."

Levi's mood soured at the mention of Cedric.

Mum went on. "And now that summer vacation is coming and she can take a break from studying, it would be the perfect time for her to visit him in Australia. Think how wonderful it will be for him to meet his granddaughter and his great-grandson."

"I'm not so sure about that."

She glanced up at him. "What do you mean? What aren't you sure about?"

"About Adria going to visit him."

"What's wrong with that?" Mum asked. "Her classes will soon be breaking off for the summer. It's the perfect time for her to pay him a visit. He's getting up in years and from what she tells me, his health isn't the best. We don't know how much time we have, and we need to make the most of it. And not everyone gets to see their great grandchildren."

Levi crossed his arms. "It's one thing if she wants to go and see him, but I don't think Owen should go."

"Why ever not?"

"I just don't think it's a good idea."

She frowned. "Do you really think she'd want to go halfway across the world without Owen, especially when it's a chance to meet his great grandfather? Of course she'll want to take him with her."

"You do realize I don't have any official sort of custody agreement in place? It's all this ad hoc business. That's been well and good while she's just over at Falconer Lodge. But what if Adria decides she wants to live in Australia and not come back? What would I do then?"

Mum stared at him. "You just said that you were in a relationship now. She wouldn't do anything like that."

"But how do we know for sure?" Levi asked.

Mum frowned. "Well, I just don't think she would. Don't you trust her?"

"Trust is one thing. Being smart is another."

"Well, if she wants to visit her grandfather, I don't see how you can stop her."

He threaded a hand through his hair. "Actually, I can. I filed for a prohibited steps order and the judge granted it. She'll have to seek my permission to get a passport for Owen and to take him out of the country. There will be no visit to Australia for Owen unless I agree to it."

"You did what? Please tell me you're joking."

When Levi stared at her without replying, Mum shook her head.

"I don't believe this. You've just finished telling me that you and Adria are dating. You're hoping to build a future together. How can there be any trust between you when you go and do a thing like this? Does she know you've done this?"

Levi shook his head.

"You're going to end up pushing her away instead of keeping her close. And what do you think that'll do with your relationship with Owen? You need to trust her if you want a future together."

Anger flared in Levi's chest. "Yes, well, you could have done with being a little bit less trustful of your husband and putting some safeguards in place so that Greg couldn't have hurt us all the way he did."

Mum went still, color flooding her face. She stood rigid as Owen slapped the water around her.

Levi regretted the words the instant they left his mouth and flew like daggers into her heart. "I'm sorry," he said. "That was a low blow. But I need to put some sort of measures in place to make sure Adria can't take Owen away from me. I want to keep him in my life."

Mum shook her head, turning away from him. She spoke to Owen in an unnaturally bright voice. "Come on, darling. Let's get you inside and dried off. I think we've had enough swimming for today."

# Chapter 44

*A*DRIA SAT AT HER desk, underlining several lines of text in her copy of Charles Dickens' *A Christmas Carol*.

The past paper essay she was working on required her to cite examples of the literary devices Dickens had used in the novella. And she was hunting down examples of personification.

Amazingly, she enjoyed it. Back in her school days, literature classes had seemed like such a chore when the teacher squeezed out every ounce of enjoyment from the text. But this was actually fun.

The doorbell rang and she got up, frowning. She'd been in a good flow. Hopefully, it was just the postman leaving a package or something.

She opened the door.

A man stood there, dressed in a smart suit with a lanyard around his neck. "Good morning. Am I speaking to Miss Adria Baines?"

"Yes," she said.

"I have a letter for you."

He pulled out a long envelope and a clipboard. "Here you go, madam. Please sign here saying that you've received this document."

"All right." She scribbled her signature on the clipboard.

"Thank you, madam. You've been served. Have a nice day."

Adria frowned. Served?

She stared at his retreating figure, then closed the door. She opened the envelope and pulled out the document.

Her heart hammered as she read the words.

IN THE FAMILY COURT

Hatbrook

Case No: FD2023/040234

Between:

Mr. Levi Falconer - Applicant

and

Miss Adria Baines - Respondent

PROHIBITED STEPS ORDER

Before: Judge Margaret Pembroke

Sitting at: Hatbrook, Surrey, on July 15th, 2024

UPON READING the application made by Mr. Levi Falconer on July 10th, 2024 seeking a Prohibited Steps Order under Section 8 of the Children Act 1989;

AND UPON considering the documents filed and representations made on behalf of the applicant;

IT IS ORDERED THAT:

Miss Adria Baines is hereby prohibited from applying for a passport or any other travel documents for the minor child, Owen Baines Falconer, born on June 22nd, 2022, without the prior written consent of this court or the further order of the court.

Miss Adria Baines is further prohibited from removing the minor child, Owen Baines Falconer, from the jurisdiction of England and Wales, or from the borough of Hatbrook, Surrey, without the prior written consent of this court or the further order of the court.

This order is made to ensure that the child does not leave the jurisdiction and that his welfare is safeguarded pending the determination of the application or further orders.

Failure to comply with the terms of this order may result in contempt of court proceedings, which could include a fine, imprisonment, or both.

Miss Adria Baines must retain this order or a copy thereof and produce it to any passport office or travel agency when asked about the status of the minor child, Owen Baines Falconer.

IT IS ADVISED that Miss Adria Baines may apply to the court at any time to vary or discharge this order upon providing sufficient evidence as to why the order should be varied or discharged.

DURATION OF ORDER: This order remains in effect until further order by the court.

The words of the letter danced and blurred in front of her eyes. Levi was trying to stop her from taking Owen out of the country? She couldn't even take him out of Hatbrook without his permission? Why would he do a thing like that? They were supposed to be in a relationship. Shouldn't they have been able to talk about things like this?

This must be about going to Australia. But he should have known she wouldn't try to take off with Owen without talking to him about it. What did he think she was trying to do?

A shiver went down her spine. How well did she really know Levi?

# Chapter 45

A LEADEN KNOT FORMED in Levi's stomach as he stepped through Adria's doorway with Owen cradled against his chest.

Adria closed the door behind him, her lovely features taut as her gaze skittered away from his.

Something was wrong.

"Someone's ready for his nap," he said, bending to nuzzle Owen's tousled curls, needing the reassuring scent and solid warmth of his son to fortify him.

When he chanced a look at Adria, her gaze was already sliding away from his.

"We, uh, we had a blast at the pool with Nana. Didn't we, buddy?"

Owen nodded sleepily against Levi's shoulder, his tiny fingers still clutching his dad's shirt.

Adria lifted her chin. "That's good. I'm glad you two had fun."

Levi flinched at the chill in her tone. "How did your studies go?"

"I didn't get much done."

The icy silence that followed was suffocating. Levi's arms tightened around his son as if Owen's solid warmth could shelter him from the arctic blast separating him from Adria.

But Adria stepped forward and took Owen from him, then settled the boy in the corner of the room with his toy cars. "There you go, sweetheart. I'll put you down for your nap in a minute." She walked to the kitchen, motioning for Levi to follow her.

"My studies were going just fine until someone came along to give me this." She held a document out in front of him.

Levi took it from her, and a wave of cold washed over him. It was the prohibited steps order. His gaze swept over the words. They looked so stark and harsh in black and white.

"You applied for this?" she asked, her voice tight.

He looked down at her, meeting her gaze. "Yes, I did."

"Why?"

"I wanted to be sure that my wishes would be consulted in case you want to take Owen to Australia."

Moisture glistened in her eyes. "Of course I would consult you. I wasn't planning on just picking up and leaving. I thought you would come with us if I were to visit my grandfather. And this isn't just about Australia. I can't even leave Hatbrook now?"

Levi swallowed the lump that had formed in his throat.

Adria glanced over at Owen and Levi's gaze followed hers.

The little boy was still busily engaged with his toys.

Adria spoke, a tremor in her lowered voice. "Are you planning on taking Owen away from me?"

Levi stared at her. "No!"

"Was that your plan all along then? Get me to trust you and then take my child away?"

"Of course not. That is absolutely not what this is about."

"There is no 'of course' about it when you can pull a move like this." She grabbed the papers away from him and dropped them on the kitchen counter.

"Listen," he said. "Let's try to be rational about this. Documents like this are supposed to keep us safe by drawing up the boundaries around us. That's all it's about, Adria. It's keeping us safe."

She stared at him. "Well, it's backfired because I don't feel safe at all."

He had no reply for her.

She took the paper and folded it up. "I think you need to leave."

"Adria—"

"I said you need to leave."

He stared at her face for a moment, then turned and walked out.

# Chapter 46

Levi walked into his living room to find Ezra standing in front of the bookshelf.

Great. His brother was the last person Levi wanted to talk to right now, when his nerves were already raw.

"There you are," Ezra said. "I've been waiting for you."

"Waiting for me? Why?"

"Mum called and told me you've gone and done something really dumb and that I need to talk some sense into you."

The sinking feeling in Levi's gut grew, but he crossed his arms and stood his ground. "What I did was not dumb. It was prudent and sensible."

"Okay," Ezra said. "I'm happy to be the neutral party here. Why don't you spell it out for me?"

Levi gestured toward the armchairs, and they both sat.

"Adria just found she has this grandfather in Australia."

"I've heard about that," Ezra said.

"And now she's talking about going to visit him and taking Owen with her. I don't think that's a good idea, so I applied for a prohibited steps order which prevents her from applying for a passport for Owen or taking him out of the country unless she gets my permission first."

He looked at Ezra, waiting for a response.

After a moment of silence, Ezra said, "I'm waiting for you to get to the not dumb part."

"What do you mean?"

"Listen, for what it's worth, I understand why you did that. You need to protect your access to your son. You don't want him stuck halfway around the world for who knows how long. Coupled with that, you don't really know Adria that well. None of us can tell what she's capable of. For all we know, she might take off over there and start a new life. You don't want that to happen, so I get why you would want to stop her from doing that. She's an unknown quantity and unknown is scary, so you think you've got to take steps to stop her."

Levi nodded. "Exactly. So, you get why I did it."

Ezra said, "Yeah, I get it. But here's why it's dumb. You said Adria's grandfather, this Cedric Fairbanks, is loaded. He's got, what, $50 million?"

"Seventy-five."

"Right, $75 million. What if he's willing to fund a legal team for Adria, and what if she decides she wants to fight you on this? It could become an ugly custody battle, with Owen stuck in the middle. Nobody is going to win. You will all be losers, Owen most of all. Is this really what you want?"

Levi went cold. There was so much more to this that Ezra didn't know, and those hidden facts made it even worse. He'd made Adria sign an NDA as a condition of his supporting her financially. With Cedric Fairbanks in her life, it was highly likely that Adria didn't need Levi's financial support anymore. She could tear up the NDA and not just fight him, but go public with all of this.

Ezra spoke up. "You've been quiet a while. Does that mean I'm getting through to you?"

Levi swallowed. "You could say that."

Ezra stood. "Then my work here is done. If I were you, I would make things right with Adria before they escalate any further. I'll be praying for you. You need it, brother."

He patted Levi on the shoulder and headed out.

# Chapter 47

After Levi left, all Adria wanted to do was curl up into a ball and cry herself to sleep. But Owen needed her. Her crying would have to wait.

For her son's sake, she'd need to wear a cheerful mask while she was ripped to shreds and bleeding on the inside. How could Levi do this to her? Had he planned this all along? When he first kissed her at Polesden Lacey, had this been in the back of his mind?

The routine of Owen's bedtime rituals kept the thoughts at bay. But eventually, he was asleep in his bed. She had to fill the hours until her video call with her grandfather later this evening.

She turned on a mindless TV show she could stare at without thinking.

Finally, it was time to talk to Cedric. Seeing his eager face fill the screen soothed her heart like cool water on a sunburn.

"It's so wonderful to see you, darling," Cedric said. "How are you?"

And now she would have to lie. "I'm all right, thanks. It's just been a long day."

"Oh, I know, you've been working hard on your GCSE English. Dickens, was it? How did you get on?"

"Not bad," Adria said. "And how are you doing?"

"Oh, I'm fine," Cedric said. "I was looking at the calendar and thinking your summer vacation must be coming up soon. I was wondering what your thoughts are about coming over for a visit. It'll be winter here in Brisbane, but it doesn't get all that cold. There's still lots to do."

Adria had been hoping to avoid that topic, but she couldn't. Not without being dishonest. And it would be cruel to keep the elderly man's hopes up. "I'm not sure we'll be able to come," she said.

"Why not? Is something wrong? Have you changed your mind about coming?"

"No, it's not that at all." She sighed. "It's Owen's father. I was served today with a prohibited steps order, which bans me from applying for a passport for Owen or taking him out of the country unless Owen's dad agrees to it. And something tells me he'd never give me that permission."

Cedric frowned. "That was a jerk move. I thought the two of you got along really well."

"So did I," Adria said.

"So what's brought this about, then?"

"I wish I knew." Adria fought against the tremor in her voice. "He just doesn't want me to take Owen to Australia. He said I can go on my own, but I'd have to leave Owen behind. And after being served with a paper like that, I'm honestly not willing to do that because I don't know what else he might pull if I leave Owen with him for an extended amount of time. For all I know, he could turn around and claim that I've abandoned him."

Cedric tutted. "Oh no, no, no, we can't have that. We can't have that at all. Listen, my dear, if you want to, I think we can fight this. I can help you with all the funds you need. We can instruct your own solicitors to take this to the courts and challenge it."

Adria thought for a moment. It probably could be challenged. But did she want to do that? She shook her head. "That's really generous of you, but I don't think the best thing to do would be to get involved in an ugly, legal fight with Owen's father. I've heard how these things can go, and I don't want to go down that road."

"Are you sure?"

She nodded. "Yes. Much as I hate to give in to this, I think trying to fight it might be worse."

"All right," Cedric said. "But it sounds like this might make things awkward for you. You said that you live in the same compound as him, didn't you?"

"Yes, I live on his family's estate." And that, too, was beginning to feel like a gilded cage.

"Well, I could help you with funds to move out, if you'd like. You can get onto it straight away. Find somewhere else, and I'll give you everything you need."

Her heart melted. "It's so sweet of you to offer that, but if this has taught me anything, it's that I really need to be able to stand on my own two feet. The reason I'm in this situation is because I've been so dependent on Levi. I'm hoping that when I get my qualifications, I can take care of myself. The best thing I can do is to be able to pay my own way. I'm not there yet, but I hope I'll be able to do that at some point. Thank you, though."

"That's very commendable of you," Cedric said. "You are clearly a young woman of character, and I'm proud of you for that. But it's not true that you don't have any money. Your father left a significant estate, and you are his legitimate heir."

Adria stared at him. "An estate?"

"Yes," Cedric said. "I'm not entirely sure of the numbers, but I believe Adrian had some property in Melbourne and various stocks and bonds. It should all amount to about £500,000. Liquidating some of it would give you some independence. The money is rightfully yours. In fact, this has reminded me, I need to go through the necessary paperwork to ensure it comes into your hands."

# Chapter 48

*L*EVI'S FINGERS STILLED ON the strings of his guitar, the last chord hanging in the air and slowly fading. He squeezed his eyes shut against the stark reality—the new song wasn't gelling. For seemingly the hundredth time that afternoon, the chorus fell flat, the lyrics ringing trite and forced.

Maybe because he couldn't write about joy and peace when he was torn up inside about the mess he'd made with Adria.

Despite his talk with Ezra and the strong points his brother had made, Levi was reluctant to cancel the court order. It was his only defense against Adria taking Owen away. Especially now that she was so angry with him.

After yet another argument about his refusal to cancel the court order, communication between them had dwindled to almost nothing. She couldn't understand why he was against his son being taken so far away. Yes, she claimed it would only be for a visit, but who knew what might happen when they were in Australia and under the influence of her multi-millionaire grandfather?

He longed to have her in his life, but their relationship teetered on the brink of collapse.

He attacked the words on his notebook with a vicious slash of his pen, then ripped off the sheet of paper, sending it to join the other crumpled drafts that littered the floor of his office.

There was a knock on his door and Mum stepped in before Levi had a chance to reply.

Everyone knew that Levi came into this room when he wanted to work without interruptions, so it was highly unusual for her to invite herself in.

Levi scowled. Just what he needed when his songwriting was already going badly.

She faced him with a scowl of her own. "I'm not going to apologize for barging in like this. I've just been speaking to Adria, and she tells me she is thinking seriously about moving away from Falconer Lodge before the autumn term starts."

Levi put down his guitar. "What? She just told you that?" Yet another sign of how they were barely speaking.

"Yes. She could be gone from here within the next two months. Are you actually surprised that after you tried to box Adria in, she decided to draw some boundaries of her own? Didn't you realize that this is exactly what would happen after you served her with that wretched court order?"

Levi stood. "Do you know where she's going? She can't take him to Australia. Not with the PSO in place."

"She isn't going to Australia. She told me she'll be looking for a place in Hatbrook so that she can stay connected with the church and so that Owen will have the chance to keep seeing me and—believe it or not—you, with as little disruption as possible."

Adria was slipping away.

Levi banged a fist on his desk. "Well, with Cedric Fairbanks bankrolling her, Adria could buy up the whole of Hatbrook if she wanted. I should speak to Oliver about drawing up an official visitation schedule so that I can make sure I get enough time with Owen. I'm not going to be a weekend and holiday father if I can help it." He pulled his phone out of his pocket.

"Can you hear yourself right now, Levi? Is this what you want your parenting relationship with Adria to be like?"

Levi looked up from his phone. "What do you mean?"

"Do you really want to be negotiating every aspect of your parenting through your lawyers and the family court? You need to drop the legal maneuvering and build a relationship with Adria that's based on trust."

"I can trust her all I want, but I can't afford to look at things through rosy eyed spectacles. We need boundaries and safeguards. That's why I'm doing this."

"Levi." Her voice cracked. "I'm sorry for not seeing through Greg, but you need to stop making everyone pay for my mistakes and for Greg's sins."

He balled his hand into a fist. "You're not making any sense. This has nothing to do with Greg."

"This has everything to do with Greg," Mum said, her voice a whiplash that stunned Levi into silence. "The son I raised had a huge and tender heart and saw the best in everyone. I know Greg took advantage of that. But not everyone is like him."

She walked up to him, pointing a finger into his face.

"You need to stop this right now, Levi. Adria is a lovely, sweet girl and you've thrown away your chance of building a family with her and Owen. Stop treating her as if she was your enemy. Have you ever heard of the phrase self-fulfilling prophecy? I don't often tell you what to do, Levi, but you need to wise up. Because you're being an absolute fool."

She spun on her heel and marched out of his office, her feet crushing the already crumpled fragments of his song.

# Chapter 49

ADRIA WATCHED OWEN AND his little friend chase soap bubbles in Eden and Pastor Noah Chaplin's backyard.

She had almost canceled this playdate. With everything that was happening with Levi, the last thing she'd wanted to do was wear a happy mask and socialize. But Owen loved playing with Linda, Eden and Noah's daughter, and it wouldn't be fair to deny him that joy just because Adria was down in the dumps.

Besides, she liked Eden. The pastor's wife had a poise and serenity that always soothed Adria. She could use some soothing company.

And maybe visiting would take her mind off Levi. Oh, Levi. She sighed. Her dream of a future with him was crumbling into ashes. How could she have been so wrong about him?

"If you don't mind me saying so," Eden said, interrupting Adria's thoughts, "You seem a bit distracted."

"Oh, am I?" Adria blinked.

"Well, you didn't answer the last question I asked you. And I asked it twice."

Adria exhaled slowly. "I'm sorry. It's just that I've got a lot on my mind."

"Anything I can help with?"

Adria bit her lip. Could she trust Eden? The pastor's wife already knew a lot about Adria's background. And Eden had shared her own story of coming to the Lord after living a sordid lifestyle.

Adria needed someone to talk to. Making up her mind, she met Eden's gaze. "Actually, yes. I've been thinking about moving away from Falconer Lodge, but I'm worried I might be making a mistake."

Eden's eyebrows lifted in surprise. "Moving away? Why? It's a lovely home, and I thought you all were getting along so well."

"We were getting along, or so I thought," Adria said. "But Levi did something, and now it's uncomfortable living so close to him."

Eden frowned. "What did he do?"

Adria glanced at the children. Good, they were out of earshot, capering around the automatic bubble blower. "He served me with a prohibited steps order because I was talking about visiting my grandfather in Australia. I can't apply for a passport for Owen or take him out of the country unless I get Levi's permission. I can't even go out of Hatbrook. He says it's because he wants to be sure I don't run off with Owen to Australia without telling him. What really bothers me is he didn't even discuss it with me. He just went straight to the family court and slapped me with this thing."

"That doesn't sound like Levi."

"Doesn't it?" Adria asked. "He's been trying to control what I do all along. First, he made me sign an NDA before I could get child support. He was being so generous, and I'd never sell my story to the press or anything like that, anyway, so it seemed silly not to sign it. Then he asked to be put on Owen's birth certificate. I was more than happy to do that because I think he should be on it. But right after, he went and got this PSO. Now I'm starting to wonder what he's really up to and whether he might try to take Owen away from me."

"I'm sure he wouldn't do that," Eden said.

"I wouldn't have thought so either until he got the PSO and then acted like he was completely in the right."

Adria's throat tightened. "I feel like I don't know him anymore. I even wonder whether he didn't have us move to Falconer Lodge just so he can have more control."

Eden touched her arm. "Oh, Adria. Surely not. I thought it was a beautiful arrangement for all of you."

"So did I, at first. But now I don't know what to think. I want to move, but I don't want to keep Owen from him. I love that Owen has a chance to know his father, to have that sense of belonging and stability. I don't want to take that away from him. But being so close to Levi...it just hurts." She wrapped her arms around her body.

Eden watched her, her expression thoughtful. "Does it hurt just because of how he went about getting the PSO, or is there more to it?"

Tears stung Adria's eyes. "Before all this, he said he wanted us to be a family."

"And you were developing feelings for him?" Eden's questions were like a physician's gentle probing. Her diagnosis was right on the mark.

Adria nodded, the tears now spilling over. "How could he say he wants to build a relationship with me and then do something like this? Or was that just another way to control what I do with Owen?"

Eden handed her a tissue, and Adria dabbed at her eyes.

Leaning forward, Eden's voice was soft yet firm. "The Levi I know wouldn't lie about having feelings for you. If he said he wants a future with you, I think he means it. But at the same time, you're not wrong to want to protect yourself if you suspect he's trying to manipulate or control you. Levi is my friend and I love him, but I think you've got every reason to be cautious."

Adria looked up. "You think so?" It was a relief to have her opinion validated, but part of her had hoped Eden would make her believe that she was misunderstanding Levi.

"I do." Eden's dark eyes were intense. "I'll tell you this since your heart is involved and you're talking about being in a relationship with him. It concerns me that Levi got the court order behind your back. It's a breach of trust. In marriage, you should be able to completely trust your husband. To know that he won't use legal or financial leverage against you. Until Levi understands that, I think you need to tread very carefully with this relationship. I hope I haven't overstepped my bounds by being so open with you."

"No, you haven't overstepped." Eden's words had chilled Adria to the core. Because her heart belonged to Levi. But how could she be with someone she didn't trust? "Thanks for being honest. But what do I do now?"

"We ask God for wisdom," Eden said. "Let's pray."

The women clasped hands and bowed their heads.

# Chapter 50

Levi walked into Elaine's office. He didn't often come here, as she tended to meet with him at Falconhurst or at the studio. But he needed to get away from home, and this meeting with Elaine was as good an excuse as any to do so.

The thought of bumping into Adria or having to face the accusing glares of his mother was enough to make him want to run off for a few hours of respite.

The receptionist met him with a smile. "Hello, Mr. Falconer."

"Hi. I know I'm a bit early."

"That's all right. She's in. Why don't you go straight through?"

"Thank you. I will."

He walked down the hall where he found Elaine's office door standing open. Her voice carried clearly into the hall.

She was probably on the phone.

He was waiting outside, not wanting to intrude, when Adria's name caught his attention, spoken in the hard, ringing tone of his manager.

"Yes, her name is Adria Baines," Elaine said. "I'm telling you, it would make the perfect story. Girls who make a career out of celebrity hookups. I've been informed on reliable authority that she ran with a crowd of girls who liked to throw themselves at celebrities at clubs and popular partying spots. Some of them just wanted their five minutes of fame, you know, getting their picture in the celebrity papers. Others wanted the perks of being seen with the right guys, getting into exclusive parties, and so on. But others, like Adria, had a different plan, and she realized she'd struck gold when she got together with a guy who actually had some integrity."

Heat surged through Levi. Elaine was gossiping about Adria. And telling some really ugly stories, by the sound of it. But maybe he had got it wrong. He was hearing only one side of the conversation, after all.

Elaine paused, probably because the other person was talking.

Levi kept his rage in check as he listened.

Elaine cackled. "I know I'm not telling you anything new. You know what these kinds of girls are like. Anyway, why do you think this girl waited almost three years before she contacted Levi? A little bird tells me that she wasn't actually sure the child was his. Around the same time she met Levi, she was involved with a different celebrity, a well-known professional athlete who shall remain nameless."

Elaine laughed again, the sound grating on Levi's ears. "Let's just say he's featured in a few Champions League teams. Anyway, she first tried with him, but the paternity results proved negative. Luckily for her, she had also been up close with Levi at the time. Rumor has it that she's—"

As she spoke, Elaine half-turned and finally noticed Levi standing in the doorway.

Color leeched from her face, and she held the phone away from her ear.

Quickly recovering her poise, she spoke again. "Listen, I'll have to call you back, all right?"

Smoothing her hair, she looked up at Levi. "You're a bit early. I wasn't expecting you until two."

"Who were you talking to? And why were you telling those lies about Adria?"

"I was just doing a little public relations, trying to shore up your reputation." She forced a smile.

"My reputation does not need that kind of shoring up."

"Well, I beg to differ. There's still a segment of your fans who may not come back to you because they think that what you did was morally wrong. They can be swayed if it's shown that you, an unworldly church kid, were seduced and pulled into this."

Heat coursed through Levi's body. "Are you seriously trying to justify yourself? On what planet do you think it's okay to win fans with lies?"

"Well, they're potentially true. This kind of thing happens all the time."

"Who were you talking to?"

"A contact of mine," Elaine said.

"Do you mean a journalist?"

Elaine shrugged. "Someone who can get a story out."

"Right." Levi's voice was a tight whisper. "Here's what you're going to do. You're going to call that journalist, or whoever they are, and recant every single word you've just said about Adria, or I will hold you personally liable for whatever story is published."

He stalked toward the door, then turned around and looked back at her. "And also, you're fired."

# Chapter 51

LEVI STORMED OUT OF Elaine's office, his ears ringing with her pleas for him to wait. He barely registered the shocked expression on the receptionist's face as he pushed through the waiting room door.

His car was parked along the road. With a flurry of movement, he slid behind the wheel. The engine roared to life and he merged into the bustling traffic.

He didn't have a destination—he just needed to distance himself from Elaine before his rage boiled over.

The venom Elaine harbored for Adria was astonishing. The lies, the dismissive tone—had she always felt this way about Adria? Why hadn't he seen it before? The advice he'd taken, the decisions he'd made about Adria—all were influenced by someone who despised her.

Elaine had subtly planted every idea—the conditional child support arrangements, the NDA, the prohibited steps order. She had sown all those seeds of distrust.

But the blame wasn't hers alone. His heart had been fertile ground. He had embraced those ideas, acted on them, treated Adria as an adversary he needed to guard against. In his misguided efforts to protect himself, he had betrayed her trust.

Adria had been nothing but cooperative, adding his name to Owen's birth certificate, giving Owen his surname, and even now, after everything, she hadn't limited his access to their son.

The night of Owen's birthday party, Adria had been so vulnerable and open, confiding her fears about how he saw her. He'd held her and told her he wanted to build a future with her. How had he gone from those tender promises to a court order?

A groan escaped Levi as the weight of his actions settled in.

"Lord, please forgive me," he whispered. "I've been such a fool and willfully blind. Forgive me for the cruel and cynical way I've behaved."

His mother, Ezra, Adria herself...all of them had tried to talk sense into him, but he'd been too bullheaded to listen.

Tears blurred his vision as he drove, the streets a blur of lights and shadows.

He yearned for a chance to make things right with Adria, though a part of him feared it was too late. The only path forward, the only way to even hope to mend the rift between them, was to rescind the prohibited steps order.

It was a risk, a monumental one. She might decide to take Owen and leave for good. But trusting her was the only chance he had to rebuild what he had shattered by his own actions. There was no guarantee she would come back to him, but it was a chance he had to take.

# Chapter 52

As the door swung open and Owen caught sight of his grandmother, he squealed with delight and wriggled free from Adria's grasp. "Nana," he shouted, toddling forward.

Adria grinned at Beth. "Looks like someone's excited to see you."

"The feeling is completely mutual. It's good to see you too, Adria. How have you been?"

Adria knew better than to pretend with Beth. "I've been better. But I'm hanging in there." Hanging in limbo with a heart that loved Levi and a head that knew they had no future. Not while he thought it was okay to go behind her back and get a court order against her.

Beth reached out and squeezed Adria's shoulder, her eyes brimming with pure love and sympathy.

Adria fought back tears. She didn't want to start bawling here on the welcome mat. "I'll be off then. Should I come to pick him up at six o'clock?"

"Yes, that'll be fine," Beth said. "Shall I give him dinner, or did you want to eat with him?"

"I'll give him dinner at home. Thanks again."

As she turned to leave, Levi appeared behind Beth.

Adria's heart lurched. He wasn't supposed to be at home today. She wasn't ready to face him. She didn't have her Levi armor on. Without it, she was vulnerable to the pleading look in his eyes and his haggard face. He looked like he'd been up half the night.

"Adria, can we talk for a moment?" he asked.

Beth inhaled sharply, then spoke to Owen. "All right, darling. Let's go for a swim before you tug my hand off."

She followed after the little boy, leaving Adria and Levi alone.

Adria steeled herself. "Sure, we can talk."

"Maybe we could talk outside," Levi suggested.

"All right."

They walked down the driveway in silence until Levi spoke. "Thanks for agreeing to talk. I'll just come straight out with it—I was completely wrong, and I'm very sorry for getting that PSO. Can you forgive me?"

The suddenness of his apology caught Adria off guard. It had come with no preamble. Just a total 180. There was no way she could have prepared for this. She stared at him. "What?"

He held her gaze. "You're free to take Owen to Australia if you wish. You can apply for his passport and travel. I won't stand in your way."

Was he trying some new tactic? "Why?" she asked.

"I made a terrible mistake when I applied for that court order. It was controlling and presumptuous, and you have every right to be upset with me. And that's not all I did."

She blinked at him. There was more?

He looked away for a moment, then faced her again. "I also hired a private investigator to check up on you and on your grandfather."

Anger flooded her. "You had someone snoop on us?"

"No, it wasn't like that." Levi held up his hands. "All the P.I. did was carry out background and financial checks."

Adria pressed her fingers against her temples. This man was unbelievable. "Why didn't you just ask me? I would have told you whatever you wanted to know."

"I know that now. I'm sorry. I was being overly cautious and suspicious of everyone."

She crossed her arms. "So, why are you telling me this now?"

His eyes pleaded with her. "I want to show you that I trust you and I'm sorry for trying to control things. And you can tear up the NDA you signed—I already have."

"But why?" she pressed. "What made you change your mind?"

Levi paused, as though searching for the right words. "I've learned there's a time to be cautious, but there comes a point when you have to let your guard down and trust—even at the risk of getting hurt."

She held his gaze. So, he was letting his guard down now after all the legal antics and siccing a P.I. on her? "Okay."

"And if it's not too late, I'd like to ask you not to move away from the lodge," he said. "I'll respect your space."

Adria closed her eyes and tried to still her mind to think straight. What could she base her decision on when it felt like there was no solid ground to stand on?

She took a deep breath. Owen. She'd base her choice on what was best for him. Moving would disrupt him. He was so happy here, and being at Falconer Lodge made it easy for him to see the people he loved every day. She looked up at Levi. "All right, we'll stay."

His face lit up. "You will? Thank you. I've missed you so much, Adria."

He stepped toward her, reaching for her hands, but she pulled back.

"No."

He stared at her, his hands falling to his sides.

It was her turn to weigh her words. "I appreciate your gestures and dropping the PSO. Staying is probably best for Owen, so I'll do that for his sake." A painful lump formed in her throat. "But I'm not sure I can ever see you the same way again. I trusted you, Levi, and now, I just don't know if I can."

He nodded, his features twisting. "I understand," he said quietly. "Thank you for agreeing to stay. I'll head back now."

As Adria watched him walk away, she longed to call him back and run into his arms. But she couldn't.

Her Levi armor had been in place after all. And she didn't know whether she could ever take it off again.

# Chapter 53

LEVI TRUDGED BACK TO the house, his last shred of hope sinking with an anchor's weight of despair.

It was over, then. Adria might have forgiven him and agreed to stay in Falconer Lodge, but their relationship was forever broken. All because of what he'd done.

His eyes burned with fatigue and unshed tears. Owen was here today. As soon as he pulled himself together, he would spend time with his little boy. The one bright spot left in his life.

Entering the house, he collected the stack of mail the housekeeper had arranged on the hallway table. The postman must have just stopped by.

He flipped through the letters on autopilot, freezing as his gaze landed on his name in Greg's handwriting.

Dropping the other envelopes back onto the table, Levi clenched Greg's letter in his fist. Why was this lying, deceiving, betraying waste of oxygen still writing to him?

Perhaps it was time to respond. Because ignoring him clearly wasn't getting the message across to Greg that Levi wanted nothing to do with him.

He should type up a letter right now. He started toward his office. Or perhaps writing to Greg wasn't enough. He could call Oliver and find out whether it was possible to stop Greg from contacting him. His solicitor could send a strongly worded letter, or maybe even write to the prison and get them to intervene.

His gaze snagged on a new framed picture that hung in the hallway. It was a portrait of Owen and Adria.

He paused, mid-stride. The sight of Adria's face brought back their talk and his bitter disappointment. He'd just been pleading for her forgiveness after betraying her trust. He'd begged God to forgive him for the many times he'd sinned grievously.

And here he was, refusing to forgive Greg.

*Forgive us our sins even as we forgive those who sin against us.*

No. Not Greg. That was a step too far, surely.

His conscience pricked at him, relentless and sharp, throwing up a verse he'd once learned by heart at Bible camp.

*Forbearing one another, and forgiving one another, if any man have a quarrel against any: even as Christ forgave you, so also do ye.*

Colossians 3:13. Levi let out a mirthless chuckle. *Lord, You are definitely bringing out the heavy guns.* No room for exceptions there.

Greg's letter seared his hand.

Levi bowed his head. "Okay, Lord," he prayed. "You want me to forgive Greg. I don't like it, but I'll try. How on earth am I supposed to do it?"

# Chapter 54

LEVI SHIFTED HIS POSITION, but the synthetic blue chair in the visitation hall of His Majesty's Prison Harrowgate wasn't built for comfort.

Cold white light streamed from fluorescent strips and the high-barred windows. Ranks of identical, starkly colored groups of chairs surrounded him. In each group, one red chair faced three blue ones.

Several visitors occupied blue seats like his. An assortment of people, different in every possible way, they all shared one thing in common. Like him, they were waiting to visit a convicted criminal. The red chairs were all empty while Levi and the others waited.

Levi glanced at their faces. Who had they come to see?

An elderly woman in a tartan skirt clutched a purse with a trembling hand while she dabbed at her eyes with a crumpled up tissue. Someone's grandmother, perhaps?

In a grouping of chairs to his left, a pretty young woman wearing a brightly patterned hijab sat with downcast eyes. At her feet, an infant slept in a car seat. Had she come to see her husband? What a place for a family to spend a Saturday afternoon. Did they make the trip here regularly?

Across the room, a young man, hardly older than twenty, sat with a stoic expression. He should be out with his friends enjoying the summer. Not stuck in this room where it was impossible to tell what the season was. Was he here to see a sibling or a friend whose life had taken a wrong turn too early? Or perhaps he, like Levi, was here to visit someone he had once looked up to. A father or uncle.

The only reason Levi had come was because his conscience refused to give him peace. He accepted that he had to forgive Greg, but it was going to be hard. He could take baby steps, though, and coming here was the first one.

The door at the far end of the hall creaked open, and a jolt swept through the guests on their blue chairs.

Levi scanned the line of gray-clad prisoners as they filed into the hall, each one moving toward his designated red chair.

There he was. Greg. The man who shuffled into the room, half-hidden by the bulk of the inmate in front of him, was a shadow of the stepfather Levi remembered. He looked like he had been here for decades instead of two years. His skin, pale and taut, hinted at difficult days with too little fresh air and long nights spent in confinement.

His prison garb of gray t-shirt and baggy jogging pants was a world away from the Savile Row suits he loved. Were they still hanging in Mum's closet? Or had she finally gotten rid of them? Even if Greg somehow got hold of one of his bespoke suits now, it would only hang off his gaunt frame.

Levi stiffened as their gazes collided.

Greg took a tentative step toward him, a faltering smile on his pasty features.

Levi stood, staring at him.

Approaching like the lowest dog in a fierce pack, Greg sat in the red chair across from Levi. "I didn't think you'd really come." His voice was hoarse, as though rusty from disuse.

"I almost didn't." It was a three-hour drive, and with every mile, a list of ways he'd rather spend his Saturday ran through Levi's mind. Such as staring at a blank wall. But he was trying to live out his faith and somehow forgive this man.

He scoured his heart for the tiniest spark of forgiveness. There was none.

Greg wiped his palms down his pants legs. "Your mother told me you didn't want any letters from me."

"I didn't. I still don't."

Greg's Adam's apple bobbed as he swallowed. "So, why are you here?"

Levi stared at him. "You want an honest answer?"

"I know you wouldn't give me any other kind."

Levi crossed his arms. "Okay. I came because the Bible says I need to forgive you. It says so in too many places to ignore. And God has been on my case about it. I don't want to, but I'm trying."

"I see." Greg smoothed his thinning hair. "I'm grateful that you're trying. I understand that it must be hard."

"Hard?" Levi echoed through gritted teeth. "You have no idea how hard. You laid waste to our family. We thought of you as our dad, but you stole every penny of ours you could get your hands on. You crushed my mother's heart. And you were trying to get away without a backward glance, jetting off to Costa Rica. Yes, Greg, it is hard."

Greg winced, dropping his gaze under Levi's verbal barrage.

Levi leaned forward. It felt so good to unload on this guy. "You know what else makes it hard? You poisoned all my best memories. I can't look at our family photos without thinking how you grinned at the camera while you were cheating on Mum and robbing us blind. That's hard."

Greg shrank into his chair.

Levi's hands were balled into fists and his breath came quickly. He'd wanted to do that for so long, to tell Greg what he felt.

But the fierce glee faded quickly.

What had he achieved? He'd come to confront the man who'd betrayed him. But all he'd done was kick a man who was already down.

Greg swiped a trembling hand over his eyes. Levi took a long, hard look at him.

This wasn't the man he was so angry with. This man in front of him had lost everything. He was incarcerated and penniless. In poor health, too, by the look of him.

Staring at him, Levi felt the stirrings of something he never expected to feel for Greg. Pity.

Levi sat back. "I'm sorry. I had to let that out before I could let it go."

Greg glanced up at him. "No, I deserved all that and more. I've had a lot of time to think in here. Too much, maybe. I know sorry doesn't even start to cover it, but I am. Sorry, that is. For everything—the money, the lies, running off...and most of all, for the pain I've caused you and your mother."

His hands shook as he clasped them together, his gaze not leaving Levi's face. "For what little it's worth, raising you and your brothers was the greatest privilege of my life."

"Thanks for saying that," Levi said. It was good to hear those words, whether or not Greg meant them. And it almost didn't matter whether he did.

Greg was paying for what he had done. Levi's bitterness accomplished nothing apart from poisoning and twisting him from inside, as Mum had said.

Twisting him until he'd become a cynical, bitter shadow of himself, and treated Adria as though she were as shady as Greg.

God had restored what Greg had stolen, and then some.

The one thing Levi didn't have—Adria's trust—he'd lost because of his own blunders. Not Greg's.

He stared across at his stepfather. "I forgive you."

Greg's eyes widened. "Thank you, Levi. That means more than you know."

Levi nodded, feeling a weight lifted from his shoulders.

# Chapter 55

LEVI STARED AT THE phone in his hand. It was two in the morning. He'd been dreading this all day and all evening.

He could have put it off another day, using the excuse of the long drive to and from Harrowgate and the emotionally draining visit with Greg.

But he needed to do this now before he lost his nerve. He had to make this call.

He glanced at the number he had written on a notepad and tapped it into his phone. A moment later, a surprisingly strong-sounding voice answered in a broad Australian accent. Cedric Fairbanks.

"Hello, Mr. Fairbanks. This is Levi Falconer speaking. I'm the father of Owen Falconer, your great grandson."

"I know who you are. Why are you calling me?"

A knot formed in Levi's stomach at the cold tone in the old man's voice. "I would like to speak with you for a few minutes, if that's all right."

"You would, would you? Well, luckily for you, I'm rather interested in hearing what you have to say, or else I would have hung up on you. And I've got some things to get off my chest, too. But I'd like to see you face to face. Do you have one of those video app things?"

"We could use Zoom or Skype, or something else."

"Skype is what I have. I use it with Adria. Yes, I'll talk to you over Skype. What's your account name?"

They exchanged details, and a few minutes later, Levi found himself face to face with Cedric Fairbanks, and feeling as though he was putting his head into a lion's mouth.

Cedric scowled into the camera. "Well, young man, what do you have to say for yourself?"

"I wanted to call you to say that I'm not going to stand in Adria's way if she wants to bring Owen to visit you. I realize I made a big mistake, and I've petitioned the court to withdraw the PSO. I'm sure you know about it."

"Yes, I know about the PSO," Cedric said, narrowing his eyes. "Adria hasn't told me very much about your dealings with her because she respects the NDA she signed. But I could guess a few things by reading between the lines. You wanted to use your money to control Adria and protect yourself, didn't you? And you panicked when you realized she doesn't need your money."

Levi's face burned. It sounded horrible when put so bluntly, but it was the ugly truth.

Cedric went on. "And I'll tell you another thing. It worried me when I heard what you were willing to do when you had power over Adria. So, what are you going to do if she decides she wants to move to Australia and bring Owen with her?"

Levi went cold as he stared at the older man. But his resolve held. "I won't try to stop her. I mean that. If she decides to take Owen and move to Australia or anywhere else, I'll find a way to maintain regular contact with Owen. I might even move to Australia myself, at least some months of the year. I'd figure it out. But I will not stand in her way."

Cedric looked at him for a long moment, his gaze penetrating the screen and boring into Levi's soul.

Finally, the old man spoke again. "Do you know why I understand you so well? It's because I made the same kind of mistakes. On a grander and more spectacular scale. When I was getting ready to marry Adria's grandmother, I made her sign a prenup. I was following the advice of my lawyers and the smart people around me. And I was trying to protect my assets. It was the smart thing to do, after all. The shrewd thing to do. But I'm not sure it didn't become a self-fulfilling prophecy. I know a thing or two about trying to use money to get what you want with the people in your life. It never ends well."

"I realize that now," Levi said.

"Good," Cedric said. "So, is staying in contact with Owen all that you want? Or is this about Adria too? Are you two in a relationship?"

Levi shook his head. "That ship didn't just sail. I completely blew it up."

"From one idiot to another, you have my sympathies," Cedric said.

"Thanks." Levi sighed. This club of bull-headed idiots wasn't one to which he wanted to belong. But he appreciated the old man's frankness.

"Thank you for calling," Cedric said, his features relaxing. "That took some courage. And you've taken my blows on the chin. You may be a fool, but at least you're a young fool. You still have a chance to change. I hope things go well with you."

Levi cracked a smile. "Thank you. But before I go, there is one thing I'd like to do for Adria. If you could help me."

Cedric quirked a grizzled eyebrow. "And now you've got me intrigued all over again. I'm listening."

# Chapter 56

ADRIA WALKED THE FAMILIAR path to the Falconers' house, her thoughts a jumble of emotions. It had been a couple of weeks since Levi had dropped the PSO, and their interactions since then were polite yet distant.

Handing Owen back and forth felt strangely like what she imagined navigating a divorce to be like, even though they'd never been married.

The long summer days slipped by without the family outings with Levi and Owen she had once dreamed of.

Adria's heart ached for Levi. She didn't bother to lie to herself about that, as hopeless and foolish as it was. Each day without him only deepened her longing, but she found herself at a loss for how to mend the distance between them. Perhaps it was a chasm too vast to ever fully bridge—a wound that might never fully heal.

She just couldn't get past how he had tried to control her, to fence her in.

At least today, she thought as she reached the door, she would have Owen to herself for a nice day together, just the two of them, like before everything changed. Before Levi came into their lives.

Levi opened the door, dressed casually in a fresh t-shirt and jeans.

Her dumb heart did a tap dance, like it always did, even when she expected to see him.

"Hi," he said. "Owen isn't quite ready, but there's someone here who'd like to see you. Can you come in for a bit?"

He went back inside without waiting for her to ask who it was.

Curious, Adria followed Levi into the lounge and stopped dead in her tracks.

There, sitting on an armchair with Owen on his knee, was her grandfather. His grin was as warm as the Australian sun.

"Surprise, my dear," he said with a chuckle. "I wish you could see your face—it's worth the ten thousand miles to get here."

"What? How? How did you—?" She was speechless.

"Mummy," Owen yelled, leaping from Cedric's knee and running to her.

She scooped him up, his familiar weight a solid confirmation that this wasn't a dream.

Cedric stood and enveloped them both in a tight embrace. He was strong for an eighty-year-old man.

"It's so wonderful to see you, my dear. Both of you. I arrived last night, and I've been getting to know this delightful little boy. We've had a lot of fun, haven't we, Owen?"

"Yeah," Owen said.

"How did this happen?" Adria managed to ask, finally finding her voice.

Cedric resettled into his armchair. "Well, Levi suggested it. And between the two of us, we cooked up the whole plot. It was a long trip, but comfortable."

"I didn't think you were well enough to travel so far."

"I'm well enough," Cedric said. "I don't plan on popping my clogs any time soon. We managed convenient connecting flights, and Beth has been spoiling me rotten since I got here."

Adria glanced at Levi, and her heart fluttered at the tender look on his face.

"I'll leave you two to talk," Levi said, then walked quickly out of the room.

"That young man and I have been talking quite a bit," Cedric said. "He's made it clear that he won't stand in your way if you decide to visit Australia, or even move there with Owen. All options are open to you."

Adria sank onto a nearby chair. "He said that?"

Cedric nodded. "I've been very open with Levi about wanting my family close. Ideally, I'd love for you and Owen to move over permanently, maybe even get involved with the business I've built."

Adria shook her head, overwhelmed. "I'm just a high school dropout still working on my GCSEs. I don't know the first thing about running a business."

Cedric smiled gently, patting her hand. "We'll figure it out. But what I want most isn't a business manager. I can hire one of those. What I do want, is my granddaughter. You, my dear, are one of a kind."

Tears welled in Adria's eyes as the magnitude of everything hit her. Cedric was here, invited by Levi, who was supporting her potential move to Australia.

Levi was prioritizing her needs and Owen's above his own doubts and fears. For the first time, she truly believed he trusted her.

# Chapter 57

Adria walked through the north wing of the Falconhurst house. She'd never been here before, but Beth had told her this was where Levi's office was, the room in which he rehearsed alone at least three hours a day. She couldn't remember whether Beth had said the first or second room on the left, but the sound of Levi singing removed all doubt.

The door stood ajar, and she paused, entranced by the raw emotion, the vulnerability in his rich, resonant baritone. It was like eavesdropping on someone crying. Her skin tingled as she listened.

"Broken chords became a melody, harmonies in a silent plea. Echoes of a prayer we've found in this sacred, hallowed ground. Hometown melody, sing me home, to the heart of where I belong."

As he sang the last line, his voice cracked, ending the song abruptly. The guitar strings jarred a discord into the silence.

Peering into the room, Adria saw Levi on a stool, hastily wiping away tears.

He caught her watching him and got to his feet. "Adria, I didn't know you were there. Come in."

"Are you sure?" She hesitated.

"Yes, absolutely. Come in." His voice was firm, inviting.

She stepped across the threshold, and he set his guitar aside. "I was just finishing, anyway. It wasn't going well. I can't write songs like Ezra, so I'm not sure why I keep trying."

"It sounded good to me," Adria said, crossing the threshold. "I won't keep you long. I just wanted to thank you for arranging everything with my granddad. It was an incredible surprise. Thank you."

"It was the least I could do," Levi replied, his voice soft. "Have you enjoyed your time with him?"

"Yes. It's been a delight seeing him connect with Owen. I don't think Owen fully understands who he is yet, but they're having a great time together."

"I'm glad to hear that," Levi responded, a smile touching his lips.

Adria took a deep breath. "I also wanted to tell you that I've made a decision. I want to visit Cedric in Australia, to go back with him when he leaves. And I want to bring Owen with me."

Levi nodded slowly, processing her words. "Okay, I understand."

"And I want it to be an extended visit. Maybe six to eight weeks," Adria added, watching his reaction closely.

He held her gaze. "All right. You and Owen need to spend that kind of time with him to build a relationship."

She took a step toward him. "I want you to come with us."

His eyes widened. "Really? You mean that?"

"Yes. I know it might be difficult with your schedule, but I'd like you there with us for the whole time."

Tears welled in his eyes. "I will make it happen, absolutely. Thank you so much, Adria. I know I've made mistakes, but I want nothing more than the chance to make things right with you."

"I think you've already started to do that. Bringing Cedric here has shown me a lot about what's in your heart."

"What's in my heart?" Levi repeated. He closed the distance between them, his gaze intense. "You are, Adria. I love you. You have the purest, most beautiful, most generous spirit I know. When I met you, I'd forgotten how to trust, how to open myself up. I was choking in fear and bitterness until you taught me how to breathe, how to trust, how to open up again. You inspire me to be the man God made me to be."

Her heart swelled. "I love you, too," she said, her voice a broken whisper. "You gave me everything."

He cradled her face in his hands, his thumbs gently brushing away the dampness on her cheeks. Then slowly, reverently, he lowered his head and claimed her lips.

# Epilogue

**L**EVI SAT IN HIS regular seat at Grace Community Church, his fingers entwined with Adria's. Owen was on a mat on the floor in front of them, busy mashing fistfuls of Play-Doh into an indiscernible blend of colors.

It was so wonderful to be worshipping God with Adria by his side.

Cedric was here too, still enjoying his visit to the UK, saying it was delightful to escape the Australian winter.

Pastor Noah walked to the front of the church. "Good morning, everyone. My name is Noah Chaplin, and I'm the pastor here at Grace Community Church. We're so glad you've come to worship with us. Before we start our regular service, we're going to do something special. There's a couple here today who wishes to dedicate their child to the Lord. Levi, Adria, Owen, would you come up to the front, please?"

Levi squeezed Adria's hand and stood. He scooped Owen up from the floor, Play-Doh and all.

They walked to the front, Levi holding Owen with one arm and the other hand holding Adria's.

They stepped into the bright lights of the main stage.

Noah smiled at them. "Welcome. So tell me, why are you taking this step?"

Levi cleared his throat. Being in front of crowds was his bread and butter, but somehow, speaking today was different.

He stepped in front of the microphone. "Over the past few months, my family, my church family, and you, Noah, stood by me when the news broke about how I became a father to this little boy. It's been a really hard and humbling journey, coming face to face with all my weaknesses and my failures."

His voice thickened. "Through it all, I have been astonished by God's grace and by how you have all showed me grace as well. And God has been so gracious in giving Adria and me this child. And despite all the mistakes we've made, Adria and I want to do things right. The first step is to dedicate Owen to God and make a commitment before you, our church family, to raise him as godly parents."

He turned his gaze to Adria, and she nodded, squeezing his hand. He faced the congregation again. "Adria is very shy about giving speeches. But before we came up, she asked me to say that she's grateful for God's amazing grace, and for how He has adopted us all into His family. And also, for how you have received her with open arms. Did I say that right, sweetheart?"

Adria blushed prettily and nodded as the congregation laughed.

Noah beamed. "Thank you, Levi and Adria. Church, shall we pray for them together? Our Lord and Father, we rejoice with Adria and Levi for the life of this precious child, Owen. Thank You for entrusting them with such a precious gift. We ask that You surround Owen with good things so that he may grow in Your will and Your ways. We pray for Adria and Levi, that You would fill them with wisdom and discernment so that they may train Owen in the way that he should go so that even when he is old, he will not depart from it. Bless this family in every way. We ask in Jesus' name. Amen."

As Noah said, "Amen," the church burst into applause and Levi didn't bother to hold back the tears that streamed down his face.

Levi's voice floated from Owen's bedroom, singing a soft lullaby. The song tapered off, followed by a quiet prayer.

The sounds took Adria back to Owen's birthday, a time that now felt both distant and vividly close because of everything they had been through since.

Levi appeared in the living room doorway moments later. "That child." He chuckled softly. "It's like flipping a light switch. One minute he's all energy, and the next, he's out like a light."

Adria smiled. "Well, he has had a busy day."

After the dedication service, the family had joined the rest of the church for their annual end-of-summer picnic. Owen had run around and exhausted himself playing with the other children.

Levi settled on the couch beside her, draping an arm around her shoulders. She leaned into his solid strength and, for a long moment, just enjoyed the bliss of being in his embrace. Despite the turbulent start of their relationship, he had truly become her safe harbor.

He dropped a kiss on her forehead. "Adria, I've been wanting to ask you something for a while, but the moment never felt quite right."

"What is it?" she asked, turning so she could see his eyes.

He didn't answer straight away, but his gaze lingered on her face, as though he were trying to imprint every contour into his mind.

Finally, he moved his body slightly away as he reached into his pocket. It was déjà vu as he pulled out a small velvet box.

The room itself seemed to hold its breath as he opened the box to reveal an oval cut solitaire diamond ring that sparkled even in the soft light of the living room.

Her breath caught in her throat as he lowered himself to one knee, caressing her face with his gaze. "Adria, I'm so blessed to be raising Owen with you. And it's so much more than I deserve, after all my failures and mistakes. I want to spend the rest of my life with you, as your husband. Will you marry me?"

Tears stung her eyes, although she had never known such happiness. "Yes, Levi," she whispered. "Yes, I'll marry you."

As he slipped the ring onto her finger, he gently lifted her hands to his lips, showering them with tender kisses.

*The End*

# But Wait! There's More!

Thank you for being a part of Levi and Adria's journey. I hope their story touched your heart as much as it did mine. If you want to dive deeper, I wrote some exclusive bonus chapters just for you:

*Bonus Chapter #1*

**Levi's Perspective:** Relive the touching reconciliation of Chapter 57 through Levi's own eyes. Find out what he was doing before Adria reached out to him and see what that moment meant to him.

*Bonus Chapter #2*

**The Wedding Epilogue:** Don't miss out on the beautiful, joy-filled epilogue that ties everything together in a heartwarming wedding scene.

Want in? Simply sign up for my newsletter and get instant access to these bonus chapters. You'll also stay updated on my latest projects and enjoy more fun extras.

https://millaholt.com/home-town-melody-bonus-chapters

*Milla Holt*

# Coming Soon: Small Town Harmony

If you loved Levi and Adria's story, the journey doesn't end here. Get ready for an all-new adventure in the Falconer family saga.

**Faith, fame, and family collide as a Christian music power couple hides a secret discord.**

Ezra Falconer's career with his brothers' band always took center stage while his shy wife Martha was content to play a supporting role in the background. That all changed when Martha's hidden talent was discovered and she became a breakout star. Shedding her frumpy image, her old-timey name, and 100 extra pounds, she transformed into the sultry and sophisticated "Morgan."

Ezra, grappling with his own career setbacks, struggles to reconcile the confident superstar with the unassuming woman he married.

Martha returns from a sell-out international tour to a marriage on shaky ground. Unprepared for the pressures of fame, she navigates new opportunities that threaten to pull her and her husband even further apart.

As they hide their crumbling marriage from family, friends and fans, Ezra and Martha are asked to collaborate on a charity album, forcing them to confront the growing silence between them. How can they rediscover harmony while they're singing in different keys?

https://books2read.com/SmallTownHarmony

# About the Author

I write fiction that reflects my Christian faith. I love happy endings, heroes and heroines who discover sometimes hard but always vital truths, and stories that uplift and encourage.

My family and I live in the east of England where we enjoy rambling in the countryside, reading good books, and making up silly lyrics to our favorite songs.

To learn about my other books, visit my website at www.millaholt.com.

Printed in Great Britain
by Amazon